THE GUILT IS ALIVE

THE GUILT IS ALIVE

HEMALATHA GNANASEKAR

KALPAZ

The Guilt is Alive

Rs. 650

ISBN: 978-81-7835-885-7

Published in 2011 in India by
Kalpaz Publications
C-30, Satyawati Nagar,
Delhi-110052
E-mail: kalpaz@hotmail.com
Phone : 9212729499

Lasser Type Setting by: Rudra Computer Graphics, Delhi
Printed at : Chawla Offset Press, Delhi

**This Book is Dedicated To
Shirdi Sai Baba For Enabling
Me To Write This Eulogy and Share
My Bereavement with You**

Contents

Preface

Long ago, when life began, our species survived by reacting instantly to the threats. The ancient humans who stopped to smell the roses became easy targets for predators. Today, the predators are mostly gone, but we are still so primed to pay attention to bad news and tend to ignore the good things happening around us.

Sivadoss, my father belonged to this very category. He was a grumbler and kept complaining constantly about one thing or the other. He failed to count his blessings and would rather count his problems.

He was blessed with five children, three sons and two daughters and I happen to be the eldest of them. Being his loving daughter, I would make an all out effort to solve all his problems, whatever it be. However, father would take the progress for granted and find a new cause for alarm.

After his retirement, when he was finding it difficult to make both ends meet, he took a drastic decision in his life. He wanted the eldest of his three sons Sampathkumar to go abroad for a job and support him financially. When he divulged this fact to me, I set about the task in good earnest and wished to fulfill his desire.

My brother on the other hand was a man of temper. First, he expressed his disinterest in leaving the family and second he was not willing to pay through his nose to the international recruiting agencies as bribes to get a job. With my prayers, I succeeded in changing his mind. Very soon, he also got a job offer in Jamaica. It was from an Indian, Narayanan, settled in Jamaica. He did not charge any recruitment fee and was also willing to pay for his air-tickets.

On reaching Jamaica, my brother realized that he had been duped. He was not given the promised job. He had a tiff with his boss and left the company. Suddenly he finds himself on the streets, penniless. I was gripped with an acute feeling of guilt, for it was me, who had coaxed him to accept the job and leave the country. Shocked beyond belief at the plight my brother had landed himself, I now felt that it was my responsibility to bring him back to India. The letter was the only means of communication then and with less access to phones, it took me nine long years to achieve this goal.

It was at this time when I was rejoicing at the reunion and thought that I was at last free from the guilt feelings that had been plugging me for nine long years that the tragedy struck. I was shattered and my life will never be the same again.

If only my father had not been too ambitious or dependent on his son! If only I had not taken my father's grumblings too seriously! If only I had not clung to my vow of non-interference ! The guilt feelings continue. The guilt is alive. Only this time, there is no way that I would recover........

1

A Bundle of Joy

I am totally in a daze and hysterical. I am clouded in skepticism, for I am still not sure whether it was me who was responsible for whatever happened to Sam in the Cameroon Hills of Jamaica, West Indies. It was actually a moment of great joy to me! I was in fact overwhelmed with joy that God had at last emancipated me from the guilt! The guilt that had been tormenting me for nine long years! When I saw Sam in the airport after nine long years, I was dumbfounded! Words failed me! Tears of joy welled up in my eyes! Controlling my emotions, I told him, "it is a dream come true! " And Sam smiled. I had never felt so happy in my life. I was enraptured! I felt as thrilled as Edmund Hillary who conquered the Mount Everest first ! And while standing there on top, reveling in my happiness, I felt strong hands - the hands of fate - shove me down, destroying my mountainous happiness! I have not yet recovered from that accident! I never will! And the same old guilt that had been plugging me for nine long years once again overpowered me! And this time, I am sure, there is going to be no remorse however much the effort from my side ! And no amount of consolation is going to soothe my turbid mind. The guilt shall always be alive. . . . .

I am Sam's sister. His full name is Sampath Kumar and his pet name at home is Babu. I am the eldest of the five children to my parents. I am followed by my sister and three brothers. My parents were childless for eight long years. And very often my mother would tell me, "we prayed to all the Gods and visited every temple in the vicinity, not sparing even the smallest one requesting Him to bless us with a child. And one fine day, God heard our prayers and you were born to us! " I was the bundle of joy to them. And when I was born, my father was away from home, in Biradilla in Madhya Pradesh. He came to see me only after eight days and when mother questioned him about this, he explained to her that he was too excited with the news and feared that something might happen to me due to evil eyes! From that moment, his love for me kept increasing steadily and continues to this day. Though I have reached middle age, I love and respect my parents tremendously, especially my father, for the love, caring and respect he holds for me. Also, with two grown up children of my own, I still look forward to his advice on all matters. On the other hand, my father who is now eighty years old, treats my problems as his own. If for some reason, I am perturbed over something, he is quick to become equally distressed and starts breaking his head with regard to solving my problem. This has often been a matter of conflict among my siblings that father was bestowing more love to me than others! And all along my life, I cherished this special love he had for me and this was a matter of pride to me!

But after what happened to Sam, I regret the love I had for my father, which made me oblige him blindly, no matter what! Probably, it was this bond of affection which resulted in the tragedy and the guilt I hold today. He has been wholly responsible for whatever happened in my life!

Of all the siblings, Babu is my favourite brother. The reason for this is ; next to me, my father was much fond of him. Father was quite excited that his third child was a boy! He believed that a son would take care of him and the family, during his old age, by stepping into his shoes. For, in those days, boys were considered as an asset to the family, while girls belonged to another family. And so when a son was born to him, my father's joy knew no bounds.

I had seen him express his exclusive love and affection to him frequently! While taking him to the kindergarten school, he would stop by and buy some biscuits and chocolates for him, and advise him to eat it during recess time. We are pure vegetarians and my parents would not even have a cake; for it has egg mixed in it. Babu suffered from Primary Complex when he was a young boy and the doctor advised father to give him an egg regularly to improve his health. This troubled father for some time but however he finally decided to feed him with an egg everyday. Our landlady was a nonvegetarian and so he had a talk with her and requested her to give a boiled egg to him everyday. In the evenings, when he heard his name being called, Babu would run into her house and have his egg. He would come out with all smiles on his face and we would then plague him with several questions with regard to its taste, colour, etc. He would then patiently answer to all our questions. After two years, we moved to our own house. We were of the opinion that this egg eating habit of his would come to an abrupt end. However, father did not wish to stop and against my mother's wishes, he continued to do this job himself. He kept a separate vessel for this purpose and fed Babu with an egg everyday till he was eight years old. Probably, it was this kind of explicit love that he had for his first son, the future caretaker of the family, that I had started to love my brother Babu over others.

When Babu was in third standard, he failed. After seeing the result on the notice board, I felt very disappointed. He had not come to school due to illness. I reached home with the bad news, and was wondering how to convey this to my people. I saw that Babu was playing happily on the rope swing secured to one of the branches of the tree. As I revealed the news to my mother, I started to cry and my mother consoled me that he would pass the next year.

2

Going Out for a Movie

I had never seen my parents quarrel. With the burden of having to take care of five children, my parents in fact had no time for disputes. But quite often I would hear father's flare-up at mother, "there is no money for that now ! Please try to understand and don't harrass me with your enhanced commitments!" And this was a regular feature at home, whenever mother requested him to foot the monthly provision bill. There was always a hankering for money in the family. And the words "no money for that" was the most commonly used statement by my father. With single income, he was always finding it very difficult to make both the ends meet and money and only money had been the single most passion in his life!

His income was just sufficient to provide us good meals and educate us in a good school. Any other indulgence was a luxury! Like the other children in the school, we never celebrated our birthdays. I remember that many a times, father would purchase school uniforms for Diwali instead of colourful frocks or pants. And we had quietly accepted the same.

It was only after we grew up into teenagers that we started to pester father to take us for outings. We would from time to time request him to take us for a movie. This job we would assign to Babu, for we were confident that father would hear his words and fulfill his wish. And Babu had a knack of getting this task done successfully. Father was then in his middle age and suffered from arthritis and frequently complained of cramps in his legs. He would summon each one of us to press his aching foot. While all of us obliged without any murmur, Babu would oppose him by yelling, “this is a very bad habit of yours!” He would also refuse to service him. Then, my sister or me would volunteer out of pity for father.

On Saturdays, father would have a short siesta in the afternoons. It was during this time that Babu would willingly go and sit by his side and start pressing his foot gingerly. While doing so, he would plead with father to take us all for a movie in the evening. Father would make a fuss and refuse to take us out, under one pretext or the other. But finally he would relent. However, he would not be having the money for this purpose. He would then take a small piece of paper and write out a note to the shop owner - from whom we bought all the provisions - to lend a loan of rupees twenty. He would then give the note to Babu and send him on the errand. In the meanwhile, we would be waiting anxiously. And after about ten minutes, Babu would return with a droopy face. We would all keep peering at his face to make out whether he was going to deliver some positive or negative news. He would then gloomily tell us that the shop owner had refused to help. While we still continued to stare at his face in disbelief, he would jump up high in the air, with a whoop of glee and proudly display the twenty rupees note. Filled with joy, we would all start for the movie.

3

An Idea to Augment Income

Whenever mother fell sick, I would go out and call the doctor who lived in the next street. On seeing the doctor, I would inform him that mother was not feeling well and ask him to drop in. He would give a brief nod. He would then promptly come to our house on his bicycle after closing his clinic. After examining mother, he would give her some large pills and ask her to swallow them two at a time. My mother would pop them into her mouth immediately. In the morning, I would find her busy in the kitchen cooking and carrying on with her usual chores.

On some days, when my father was at home, after attending to mother, the doctor would sit with him and have a chat. Once, when I had gone on a similar errand to the clinic, the doors were open, but the doctor was not in. After a thorough search, I found him sitting in the adjoining tailor's shop, learning to fasten a button to a shirt. From then on, whenever I went to call the doctor, I found him in the tailor's shop, where he would be learning his new trade and one fine day, to my surprise, I found him at the sewing machine stitching a shirt.

During one of his visits to our house, I saw him discussing something very seriously with my father. Both of them were talking in hushed tones, and so in spite of lingering around them, I could not even get the gist of it. However, I learnt about it the next day, from my mother. She told me that father was getting a loan of Rs. 800 from his office to purchase any household gadget and he was planning to buy a sewing machine. Though a civil engineer working in a government organization, my father could never make both ends meet and there was always an acute shortage of money at home. He had always wished to do some sort of business to augment his income. He had made many an attempt to do some construction jobs privately, but my mother was against it, as it required his staying away from home. She advised him to take care of the children and be satisfied with what God had given. When the doctor told him that he had learnt tailoring and that he could stitch blouses for the ladies, my father was ready to offer him help by purchasing a sewing machine. He also advised him to carry out his part-time job from our house itself and a memorandum of understanding was reached between them that they would share the earnings equally.

On the day the sewing machine arrived, a small crowd had gathered, curious to know what we were up to. My mother explained it all to them. After this, many of our neighbours also started attending tailoring classes regularly. We children were not allowed to touch the sewing machine and hence waited eagerly for the doctor to come, so that we could have a glimpse of the machine, when the doctor worked on it.

The summer vacations were coming to an end and it was time for school to reopen. This year, father bought material for the uniforms for all my brothers and they were very thrilled. The next day, our doctor arrived sharp at 11 a. m. We stopped our games abruptly and surrounded the doctor to watch him operate the new sewing machine and stitch the half pants and shirts for my brothers. He took out the sheet on which he had noted down the measurements and cut the navy blue cloth dexterously. My mother reminded him from the kitchen about father's advice that the uniforms should be made a little loose – for children grow very fast and they should be able to wear it at least for another two years. The doctor laboured over the job, cutting and stitching the uniforms and one fine day it was ready. He waited for my father to return from office. On his arrival, he handed over the uniforms which he had so painstakingly sewed. My father was very anxious that my brothers try them out immediately. He summoned my brothers one by one and asked them to wear them. Babu, with joy writ large on his face, tried on his new outfit very carefully so as not to soil it, while the rest of us stood at a distance watching the reaction on my father's face. On seeing my brother in his new uniforms, it was with great difficulty that we were able to muffle our laughter. The pants were so loose that my brother could have easily inserted both legs through one side of the pant itself. It was the same with my other two brothers' uniforms as well. The doctor knew that he had committed a blunder but he concealed it by telling us that father had wanted the uniforms to be stitched very loose. However, he assured father that he could alter them suitably. This he did in great earnest, several times, until the pants acquired a distinctive shape. My brothers were reluctant to wear the Bermuda shorts to school and their trauma was relieved when father finally told them to use it at home and promised to have another pair tailored with the help of a proper tailor.

But the doctor did not give up. He attended tailoring classes and practiced on our sewing machine everyday. One day, he did not turn up and after a few months, we heard that the doctor had got a job in a garment factory that exported their goods. The sewing machine remained in our house for quite a few years gathering dust and grime. However much my father tried to convince my mother to learn tailoring, she would not budge, telling him that she had no time for it. One fine day, father sold the sewing machine to his friend for half the rate and we children were happy about the extra space we gained at home.

4

No Value Without Money

After I completed my tenth standard, father sent me to shorthand and typing classes. To me whatever father said or did was the best and so without any protest, I attended the classes. It was a hectic time coping with both school studies and the short hand lessons.

I don't know the exact reason why I was too much attached to my parents. I loved them and wished to please them in every possible way I could. Probably, it was their extraordinary love they had for me, that I wished to keep them happy. My father often told me that "if you don't have money, no one would respect you. Friends and relatives would shun away from you. Money was everything in life. Without that, a man has no value!" Hence, at a very young age itself, I realized that the best way to please my parents was to make them rich. And for this I was bent upon doing anything in life.

As we were all growing up, the demands on my father were increasing and the quarrels between my parents over money were increasing too. Sometimes, mother would get sulky and not talk to my father. At such times, I would intervene and tell my mother, "ma, one day, I would go out for a job and earn much money. You can then spend it as you like. " This would bring solace to her.

When I passed my plus two board examination, father was not interested to send me to a college. Instead, he found me a job in a research centre, nearby to my house. Hence in 1984, at the young age of eighteen years, I was working as a steno-typist for a monthly salary of Rs. 300/-. I was head over heels when I received my first salary and gave the cover to father, who asked me in turn to give it to my mother.

Though I was happy that I got a good job at a very young age, soon a new problem cropped up. The director of the company to whom I reported was an old and short tempered man and kept yelling at me for each and every thing. His frequent bickerings were untolerable to me. I was basically a shy and soft spoken person. I would not even raise my voice when I spoke to people and receiving such blasts from him was making me hate the job. After a period of two years, I was planning to leave the job.

When Babu heard about this, he was as usual angry with me. "You must come out of your shell! You must be outspoken and not be filled with inferiority complex! No use in just being a book worm. " He chided me. Though younger to me, he would readily offer his advice to me on all matters. At times, his intervention would lead to a fierce argument between us.

However, he liked my younger sister Usha, more than me. While going to school, Usha would assist mother in packing up all our lunch boxes and also carry it for us to school. During lunch hour, all of us would queue up in front of her class to collect the same. Usha was an ace cook and she would prepare tasty meals for all of us. Babu was always disgusted with me because I hated to do housework. I enjoyed reading rather than doing house work. "You would have problems in your mother-in-law's house" he would curse me. And I would tell him that God was with me and he would take care of me.

I had a great belief in God. I would spend a few minutes everyday, offering prayers to Him. Early in life, I learnt that one who does wrong would be punished by God and vice versa. So, I always tried to be kind and humble to others. If for some reason, I fought with my friends or siblings and hurt their feelings, I would stand in front of God and seek His forgiveness.

5

The Business Woman

Day by day the family expenses were mounting. Everyone in the family was harassing me about my decision to leave the job. Some of my relatives even rebuked me, “your father had been struggling all the while bringing you five children up. Can’t you help him by sharing his burden at-least till your marriage?” I sharply retorted that I was busy preparing for my B. A examination and once the same was over, I would try for another job.

My mother however had a different opinion. She would tell my father, “a gentleman would not prefer to send his wife for a job and why do you struggle so much in finding a job for your daughter ? Instead see a nice bridegroom and get her married!” But this would only fall on deaf ears and father would say, “I want her to stand on her own feet and be independent in life! I shall try and get her a government job first. It will then be very easy to find a bridegroom for her!”

Father had stirred in me an interest for a government job. On rainy days, when he saw me leave for work, struggling with an umbrella he would tell me, "I am not sending you for a job just for money! I want you to become bold and also get some experience ! This will help you in the future when I try to get you a government job in my organisation where I work. " And on days when I had complained to him about the Director's railings, and my intention to resign the job, he would tell me, " just bear with everything for a few more months and things will fall in line very soon ! In a government organisation, no boss would raise his voice against his subordinates and would treat them with kindness! Apart from a good working environment, there is also job security! There is nothing like a government job!" And thus began my quest and a craze for a government job. Father's constant bragging of his government job where apart from the monetary benefit, one enjoyed a pleasant working atmosphere, made me set the same goal in life. I must somehow try and get a government job very soon and that too in my father's organisation, where he worked.

However, I could not wait any longer. One fine day, I handed over my resignation letter, after seeking father's permission. I did not pay any heed to the frequent criticisms that came my way and instead spent my time preparing for the examination. Once my exams were over and when I was a little relaxed, I realized that I had indeed taken a drastic decision. Seeing that my parents were always struggling for money, I felt bad in leaving the job. An intense desire to be of help to my parents in any possible way was kindled in me. I pondered over it for quite some time until an idea crossed my mind.

My father presented me a diary on New Year's Eve of 1985. This was a different kind of diary and was titled *The Ideal Home Diary*. It contained small tips on every subject and I treasured it as a reference book. As I scanned the pages, I was rather thrilled to read the information on manufacturing detergent powder and herbal shampoo. After reading it, an idea struck me. This was indeed a very good opportunity to make money! Immediately, I envisioned myself as a busy businesswoman, who made it to the top, by dint of hard labor. I spent the whole day, taking down notes from the book and chalked out a plan for carrying out the project. That night while going to sleep, I experienced a unique satisfaction of having accomplished a great task, and it is not for nothing that it is said "well planned is half done". The list of chemicals that were to be procured was now ready. The next day, I pleaded with mother to buy me some chemical powders from the market, through our shop owner's assistant, a young boy. I had also asked her to get me some wood ash from our neighbour, who still used wood as fuel to cook. It almost took a whole week to gather all the resources to begin my business. *'Selling my products will be no problem, as the shop owner will readily agree to sell them'*, I reassured myself.

I selected a secluded spot where I would not be disturbed. In front of me were half kilo packets of various chemicals and a huge quantity of wood ash. Using a measuring cup, I mixed the chemicals in the right proportion and began to sieve them over a thick sheet of paper spread out in front of me, in order to remove any lumps and also to get a fine mixture of the detergent powder. It was only an hour after commencing my job, when all of a sudden, I felt a sharp pain in my shoulder joints which was probably due to continuous movements involved in sieving. In a short while, my hips and back also began to ache. *'But this can't be an excuse for quitting the work. Hard work alone yields best results. When the business expands, I can always employ a few women, and that is not a big deal'*, I told myself. By afternoon, the detergent powder was almost ready. After dusting off the thin layer of chemical coating from my dress, I stretched my hands and legs to relieve the pain.

After having a quick bite, I started making the herbal shampoo. This was much easier and all I had to do was mix the wood ash in water and heat it for a while. After cooling it, I added the necessary chemicals and the shampoo was ready to be stored overnight, after which it could be used. It was dusk when I was done with my job. That night I writhed in acute pain. However, I did not complain, for fear that my parents would advise me to abandon the project. I closed my eyes, yearning for daybreak.

It was an unforgettable day indeed. I woke up very late and my folks had already left. It was 10 am, and the maid servant came in. I handed the detergent powder to her, and told her to wash the clothes with it. When she dried out the clothes, I found that the grease marks and the grime were still present. I learnt that the powder did not foam well and hence the stains were reluctant to leave the clothes. Surely, no customer was going to like it! But I did not regret relinquishing this project, for the body ache I suffered the whole night, alerted me to the fact that, this was not the kind of job that I could handle independently.

But I still had a chance of success. I lifted the bottle of shampoo and observed a thick layer of wood ash sediment at the bottom. I decanted the clear liquid into another bottle and stored it in a corner of the bathroom. I wished to wash my hair with it the next day to test its quality. It was just then, that my little brother Ramesh returned from school. On seeing him, I changed my mind. Of all the siblings, he was my pet and eight years younger to me. I adored him, mainly because he would obey me with implicit faith. I explained to him - my first customer - with great enthusiasm, all about the shampoo, and he was impressed with it. He also agreed to use it immediately. I called him into the bathroom and sat him on the floor. Since it was a home-made herbal shampoo, I was quite liberal and took a handful of it and began applying it on his head. On seeing the handful of shampoo, my brother expressed his fear that it could burn his eyes and I reassured him that it was a herbal one and was harmless. Unfortunately, the shampoo did not form any lather either. So, I poured out some more and started scrubbing his hair exerting extra pressure. But it was not of much use and there was not enough lather. By now I was under stress by the utter failure of my project and lifting up the bottle, I emptied it fully over his head, hoping that this huge quantity would work up some foam. Sensing that my attempts were in vain, I tried to calm myself. Slowly, I rinsed out his hair with water and with it the idea of becoming 'a big business woman'. Babu once again criticized me for giving up my job and wasting both time and money in such worthless projects.

6

On the Day Father Retired

At last, when my attempts to become a business woman failed, I decided to go out for a job. Once again father found me a job, through one of his friends. My new boss was even worst than the previous one. He would not tolerate even a single mistake in my typing work and I was scared out of my wits, whenever I went to him. Slowly, I improved in my job and attained very good experience in taking down dictation and typing the same. Two years passed by and still there was no news from father regarding his promise of getting me a government job. My fervent prayers for a government job, that too in my father's organisation continued.

Very soon, my father realised that things had changed. He had in fact guessed wrong. He had thought that getting me a job in his organisation was going to be a child's play and had tempted me into it. Though he had been meeting all the concerned higherups, they only told him that there were procedures to be followed for a government job and one must first of all register in an employment exchange. Tests would be conducted and only if I passed in that, I would be qualified for the interview. Recommendation did not work here.

One evening, I returned home very tired from work. I had a lot of typing work to do and hence suffered from body ache. But the moment my father revealed the good news to me that there was a vacancy in his organisation for the post of Stenographer, I became too excited and all the pain disappeared at once. But seeing my excitement, he warned me, "it is only a temporary job and once the contract period is over, you will be sent home. It is upto to you to decide!" Further, he told me that if I happen to be lucky, the post may be confirmed. Taking a risk, I resigned my job and joined my father's organisation in the Accounts Department, believing that my wish had at last been fulfilled.

I went to work happily, hoping that my job would be confirmed very soon. My father worked here as a Civil Engineer. Occassionally, I would see him enter our department with files to get financial concurrence. I would feel too shy to talk to him.

It was New Year's Eve. The year was 1990. But there was no joy in my mind. I had no new year resolutions, nor did I plan any celebration. I was very sad ; for father was to retire on 31st of January this year. I was worried about the fate of our family. Even with his full salary, maintaining the family was difficult and now with his pension, I wondered how he was going to manage.

Besides that, I was also filled with tension regarding my job. Would my job become permanent ? Or would I be sent home after my contract period is over ? Since I was working in the Accounts Department, I was given all the retirement papers of my father for typing. Everyone appreciated the fact that it really is an unusual coincidence that a daughter is preparing the retirement papers of her own father. The whole of January

I was busy typing the retirement papers of my father. And on the day of his retirement, I left early from work, without attending his retirement function, with tears flowing all the way.

While my father's retirement did not affect my other siblings in any manner, it changed my life topsy turvy. May be because I was the eldest in the family, I worried a lot more than the others. Exactly after six months, when my contract came to an end, I was sent home. Suddenly, I felt helpless and anxiously waited for something good to happen.

My father got a lumpsum amount of Rs. 98,000/- on his retirement day. He made it clear to my mother that he would never touch this money at any cost and it was fully reserved for my marriage. Further, he told her that she had to now maintain the family only with the meagre pension and not pester him for money. My mother took his retirement very lightly. Seeing my father's gloomy mood, she said, "God is there to take care of our family!"

7

Fun with Camera

By this time, Babu had completed his Diploma in Airconditioning and Refrigeration. He had got a job in one of the reputed companies. He was finding it very difficult to travel everyday as his work place was out of Chennai city, in Tiruninravur. Sometimes, he stayed back in his office and worked during night also. Babu always had interesting stories to tell us. We would all have a hearty laugh on hearing his humourous stories. Once he told us that while working in the night, he saw a ghost. He vouched on the fact that ghosts do exist and shared his experience with the ghosts. He had a knack of keeping us all enthralled with his numerous stories.

If at all Babu had a weakness in him, it was his short temper and superiority complex. He always thought very high of himself. At home too, he would always wish to have the last word and kept commanding everyone. This often resulted in frequent tiffs between us. Seeing me spend so much time for prayer he would yell, "what are you chanting bla bla bla always ? You could spend your time more usefully. You have been praying all these years, does God ever hear your prayers?" On hearing his ungracious words, I would flinch. In a way, he was right, I would think. I had been praying for a government job for almost six years now. But God had not fulfilled my wish. All my attempts to get a government job only met with failure. I started feeling frustrated over this. However, I did not wish to give up, no matter what. I continued to pray to God, with added fervency.

Though Babu was only twenty -one years old, he was filled with pride and egoism. I would advice him that these were ruinous feelings and he had to change himself. But he would hardly pay any heed to my advice. In fact, I had to constantly keep reminding him that I was his elder sister and he should listen to whatever I say.

As a result of his bad temper, he could not continue working in one particular place for a long time. After having some tiff with the Managing Director, he resigned his job. Then, he joined a big hospital in Chennai as an AC technician.

One evening he returned home excitedly. He had brought home a camera and we were all seeing a camera for the first time. We stopped doing our work, and ran to see the camera. He started showing off by clicking several photos in quick succession. Finally, he gave the camera to mother and asked her to take a snap of all her five children sitting together. Though mother was so thrilled to hold a camera in her hand, she informed him that she did not know how to operate it. Babu then sat down beside her and explained to her about the right way of using the camera. Confidently my mother grabbed the camera from his hands and said, "ready one, two, three. . . . , when all of a sudden, my second brother Raghuram continued, "run" and we all burst out laughing. Babu always enjoyed it this way. He liked the whole family to sit, chat and laugh together.

One dull Sunday morning, we were all sitting in the hall and discussing with father, on how best we could be of help to him in enhancing the family income. Just then, we heard the unbolting of our gate and eagerly peeped out. A young man full of smile on his face was walking towards us. He was a total stranger to us and when he introduced himself to father, he at once recognized him. Father then told us that he was Seenu, who was the son of the landlady, in whose house we were staying for rent fifteen years ago. I had a faint memory of him, while my siblings could not remember him as they were all toddlers then. While he kept talking to father enthusiastically, we were looking forward to his making an early move. Slowly, Seenu turned to Babu and struck a conversation with him. He told him that he likes to meet old friends and talk to them and that is why he had come to see father after fifteen long years by somehow tracing out his address. While we were muffling our laughter at this strange fellow, Babu listened to him keenly. And when he told Babu that he was working as an AC Operator, his interest in him was further aroused. They continued to chat in earnest for a long time and finally Seenu stood up and invited Babu to accompany him to have some tea and snacks. Though Babu had just woken up and had not even brushed his teeth, he went along with him, just to please him. When the two left the house, my youngest brother Ramesh ran after them with the helmet which Seenu had left behind. But Seenu coolly said, “keep it there, I shall come back!” And our heart sank.

8

Copper Lamp which Glittered Like Gold

Father was worried about the mounting expenses and his inability to cope with the same. When mother advised him to go out for a part time job, he curtly refused telling her that he had to first of all get a government job for me and then find a good suitor, after which only he would take up any other job.

Being jobless at home was pricking my conscience, for the quarrels in the family between my parents were becoming more frequent. To add to this, Babu was having problems with his new boss and was thinking of leaving his job too.

I attended many interviews and since father was at home, he too accompanied me. But I did not succeed in getting any job. However, I was not let down by this fact. Instead I spent my time preparing for my MA examination, which was due in May. Apart from this, day in and day out, I stood in front of God and vigorously prayed for His blessings for a government job.

One evening Babu returned home and gave us the shocking news that he too had left his job. Though all workmen and technicians in the hospital where he worked, were compelled to wear uniforms, Babu did not wish to oblige. This resulted in a wrangle between him and his boss and finally Babu tendered his resignation and left his job. Now he was also sitting at home.

Father was distressed that all of us were sitting at home without a job. A crazy idea came to his mind suddenly. One day, he went to meet an old friend of his and requested him to give him some petty construction jobs. The old friend was once a petty contractor, who was at father's mercy when he was in service. With father's favour and support, he had grown up in life as a big contractor. He told father, "I shall revert back to you very soon regarding this!" He never did.

I was frustrated and wondered why nothing good was happening to any one of us. I decided to bring about a few changes in the method of my offering prayers to God. There was an old copper lamp in the loft. I removed it from there and scrubbed it as hard as possible until it glittered like pure gold. I started lighting this lamp every evening. Probably, the light from the lamp would dispel darkness of our lives too. God would be pleased with me and this would result in my getting a government job very soon.

In spite of the frugal life that we were leading now, father did not discourage me when I told him one day that I had to buy some books for my M.A. Examination. However, his snide remarks hurt me. He said, "no use of studying M.A. alone ; you must be bold and outspoken too!" I did not wish to retort him.

While my father was bent upon getting me a job, everyone else in the family was getting fed up and losing their patience because of my delayed marriage. My sister Usha was worried that no one was coming to see me and one fine day she came and stood near the door and said, “come, come, please do come!” as though she was addressing the guests! When I asked her what she was doing, she told me that she was in fact play acting. “I have become mad because no man is coming to see you and get married to you!”, she said. She was so interested in marriage and wished that I clear the way for her quickly.

9

Looking Desperately for Some Help

One day, my aunt, father's sister came home along with an old man. She told us that the old man was a family friend of hers and was a good astrologer. His prophecy always turned out to be true. After spending a few hours with us, he invited us to his residence for a special puja to be performed for my early marriage. While leaving, he said, "don't worry child. Your horoscope is too good. Very soon, you will get a good job and also get married to a nice gentleman!" His reassuring words brought solace to my turbulent mind.

One occupation, all of us indulged in, was to wait eagerly for the postman. Father would be whiling away his time in the portico reading the newspaper and only after seeing the post man pass by our road, would he go to have his bath. One day, I was walking around with my book in hand, cramming for my exams. Feeling exhausted, I sat down on the portico to rest for a while. Our dog Jimmy happily came and stood near me and as usual I started patting its head and it enjoyed my continuous rubbing. My mood was so dull and I expected something good to turn up all of a sudden. In fact, I wanted the postman to deliver some letters to me. Within a few minutes, I saw the postman pass by. He stopped in front of our gate. However, he went to the opposite house to deliver some letters to them. This irked me so much. I continued sitting there dreaming. Just then, I saw a crow flying with a piece of bread in its mouth. It comfortably perched itself on our gate and started nibbling at the bread. My disturbed mind started to act in a cruel manner, all of a sudden. I wanted to grab the bread from the crow and feed Jimmy with it. I picked up a stone and hurled at the crow. The crow flew away and I ran to grab the bread from there. While Jimmy relished the bread, wagging its tail, the crow flew away ; surely cursing me. But I did not care!

Next to me, if at all any one cared about the welfare of the family, it was my brother Babu. He too was trying for a job vigorously. If an opportunity came his way, he was also prepared to go abroad for this. Very soon, he was offered a job in Dubai. He had made all the arrangements for his travel to Mumbai, where he was to take a medical test. If he was selected, he would be asked to proceed to Dubai from there. Mother was reluctant to send him abroad. However, I explained to her about the advantages of his going abroad. Babu would earn a lot of money and send it back home. He would make our family rich and that her frequent quarrels with father would also come to an end. Finally, I was able to convince her and she said that he could go anywhere but he ought to return after two years and settle down in Chennai.

I was sad on missing him too. But what was to be done ? With father's retirement, poverty had set in and only Babu's going to Dubai would uplift the family. Tearfully, we bid good bye to him. Father and Raghu accompanied him to Central Station to give him a send off. There was no telephone in our house then and so we could not communicate with him in any way. Five days passed by and there was no news from him still. On the fifth day, I saw an auto stop near our house and while wondering who it was, Babu came out with his suitcase, beaming with a smile. He then explained to us that the medical tests were over and the results would be intimated by telegram. Somehow, I was so happy to see him back. Despite the indigence prevailing at home, I could not bear a separation in the family.

For the next few days, Babu was entertaining us with stories about his Mumbai trip. He told us that since he could not book his return ticket in advance, he was forced to come in an unreserved compartment. In the middle of the night, a few ruffians armed with knives entered his compartment. They threatened the passengers with their knives and demanded them to part with their cash and jewellery. Being a young boy, Babu was spared. Early in the morning a man sitting opposite him, woke up with alarm. His suitcase with a cash of Rs. 3000/- in it was missing. The man however was not concerned about the loss of his money. He was worried about his pant and shirt which he had removed the previous night and safely kept inside the suitcase. With only a Dhoti and a buniyan, he got down to the platform , looking desperately for some help.

10

The Summer Rain

I had felt happy that Babu would get the Dubai job and make our family rich. But suddenly I lost all hope! For, the Overseas company in Mumbai did not revert to him. Also, his other numerous attempts for an overseas job only met with failure. One reason for this was due to Babu's adamancy. He was not interested to pay any fees to the recruiting agency and argued that he should be selected purely for his merit.

A constant fear always kept lingering in my mind. I was so scared about my future. The fact that both marriage and job were getting delayed, was so unbearable. Negative feelings engulfed me. Is there a God or not ? If so, why does he not fulfil any of my wishes ? Will I have to undergo only suffering all my life ? If only I was born in a rich family! I could buy anything I desired! Or atleast, I should have been born in a poor family, where I could have led a carefree life without bothering about the future and leading life one day at a time. A middle class family is a curse to be born in! One has to keep struggling, yearning for the comforts of the rich people and could not lead a low class life either. Lack of money was only the thing that my parents ever talked about and how helpless I was.

I tried hard to concentrate on my MA examinations which were due in the month of May. I hardly had a fortnight to complete my preparation. April was generally considered to be a month of peak summer in Chennai. One morning, the weather was extremely hot. But during the mid day, there was a sudden change in the climate. Dark clouds started gathering in the sky and a cool wind was blowing. And within a few minutes, rains started lashing down. I sniffed the pleasant fragrance of the earth and let myself get wet in the rain. The rains were unrelenting and continued for the whole day. It poured continuously for the next few days too. This was very unusual and father complained about the sudden change in the atmosphere and weather conditions.

This summer rain had a soothing effect and it calmed my mind. It removed the fear I had about my future and made me think positively. On the days that followed, it continued to rain in torrents. One morning, I was enjoying the coolness in the air and walking in the puddles of water in the garden. Just then, I heard a loud and authoritative voice call out, "Hemalatha Post". I ran out and collected the rose envelope from the postman. It was an interview letter from a government organisation. I was seeing this postman for the first time. He had come on transfer from Kancheepuram and had a big red vermillion mark on his forehead. Since he had undergone an operation, he could not even ride a bicycle and went around by foot, unmindful of the rains or the heat.

The following week, I attended a written and typing test and waited for the result. After a few weeks, the same old postman gave me the second rose envelope. This time, it was a call letter for an interview. After attending the interview, my father volleyed me with several questions as to what they had asked me in the interview and how I had answered them. I patiently told him everything. A few weeks later, once again the postman handed me the third rose envelope. This time it was for the medical test. My father eagerly kept waiting for the post man everyday. One day, he was away on an errand and missed the postman by a few minutes. However, he spotted him handing over a letter to somebody across the street. Father scurried across the street to meet him and the postman angrily said, "if there is any letter, I shall give it to you , Sir! You don't have to worry about it!" My father returned dejectedly.

11

Fulfillment of a Dream

When there was no response even after a month, I started to panic. Was anything wrong with my health ? For it was only after the medical check up that the letters stopped coming to me. But my doubts were cleared very soon. One Saturday, my parents were away to attend a function. The same postman came to our house and handed over a large envelope to me. I anxiously tore open the envelope. It was my appointment letter requesting me to join at my convenience. When my parents arrived in the evening, I told father the good news and he was so thrilled. And mother said, "your father retired from government service in January and by December God has helped us, by giving you a government job.

It was not just me who rejoiced at my appointment order, but my entire family was happy. My sister Usha wished to discontinue her studies after passing her plus two, due to paucity of funds. But now she became too excited and said, "well, I can do my B. A Economics by correspondence now!" Money began to flow in. Father's happiness knew no bounds. He felt relaxed and happy now. I felt exulted in the fact that I could make my father happy. At last, I was able to do it! I was able to fulfil my father's wish and be of help to my family monetarily. I could help my family in erasing the poverty life.

For the first time in my life, I realized the powers of prayer. I understood that intense prayer, offered to God in good faith brought about the desired results. Belief and trust in Him, accompanied with fortitude could move mountains. However I learnt this lesson the hard way in life. For one had to possess tremendous patience and courage to withstand all hardships that come in the way! Thank you God, I prayed once again with tear filled eyes.

The next day, when father saw the postman and ran behind him, he said, "I have given the expected letter to your daughter yesterday!" And my father said, "I know that", and handed him a ten rupee note which he accepted thankfully.

So, after a struggle of nearly six years and eleven months after my father's retirement, during the fag end of 1990, I got a government job in M/s. Hindustan Petroleum Corporation Limited. It was one of the best jobs on earth. The working atmosphere and ambience of the work place was really magnificient. I stepped into a royal and grand life, I had never known before. Respect and love from my own people gave me immense joy. I made people happy with my money. Each one had a wish of their own and I happily fulfilled it for them. However, I did not give up my prayers. My prayers did not make me feel proud and haughty. It annihilated the ego feelings of being independent and taught me to be more humble and kind.

Life was enjoyable for the next two years. When I gave a hefty sum to my mother every month, she was too excited. Also, I availed a vehicle loan from my office and purchased a motor bike for Babu. He was so thrilled to be moving around in his new Hero Honda stylishly. Now with the monetary factor taken care of, I worried about the next important thing in my agenda - my marriage. This was a constant matter of worry for my mother. My father now happily gave advertisements in the *Hindu*, and also registered in several match making centres.

Once in a month, on Sankat Chaturthi Day, mother would string a beautiful garland made out of grass. Father and I would take it to the temple and perform special *abhishekam* to Lord Vinayaka to remove all hurdles for an early marriage.

12

The Marriage Conditions

Though Babu got job offers in different companies, he could not continue working for a long time in one particular place. For very soon, he would get frustrated for one reason or the other and resign. Finally, he decided to start a business of his own and requested father to give him Rs. 10,000/- to set up his business. Father refused to help him. But mother was prepared to help him by pledging her jewels. However, Babu abandoned his business idea and was on the look out for another job.

Once again, my prayers to God for a good husband, met with success. I had given God a list of conditions that He should have in mind while selecting a husband for me. He should be someone living within fifteen kilometers from my house. This would enable me to make frequent visits to my family. He should let me pray to God for almost an hour everyday. He should let me keep a servant and a cook at home and not let me do housework.

Many men came to see me and were also willing to marry me. However, for some reason, I could never give my concurrence to my parents. This irked my siblings. Once again I turned to God and prayed, "Oh God! Why am I dissatisfied with the different alliances that are coming on my way. I shall give you fifteen days time. During this time, any man who comes to see me will be the person selected by you and I shall marry him wihout offering any comments!"

It was during this time that one Mr. Gnanasekar came to see me along with his father. Everyone in the family liked him but me. And the reason I gave my people for not liking him was that he was fat. On hearing this, Babu got provoked. He screamed at me, "Hem, you must feel ashamed of yourself! You are twenty six years old and still not married. If you were married at the right time, you would be the mother of two children by now. You keep acting in a childish manner ; refusing all the alliances, giving one reason or the other. We are also getting old and how long do we have to wait. If you don't give approval to this alliance, I bet you will never get married in this life!"

I took Babu's outburst rather seriously. What if I am never interested in any of the men who come to see me! Probably, this could be the man selected by God Himself, for he had come during the fifteen days time that I had given God for carrying out my wish. I simply gave my concurrence to my parents without resentment. My marriage with Mr. Gnanasekar was fixed on 30. 8. 1992. Just a week before my marriage, I started feeling so depressed at the thought of leaving my family. My youngest brother Ramesh who felt very sad on missing me started treating me with variety of snacks every evening.

After marriage, I nicknamed my husband as Hardy after the character in "Laurel and Hardy". He did not oppose to this. He also tried to transform me. I had always been a shy and a reserved person. He gave me freedom and brought me out of my shell. On April 11, 1993, Vadakappu, a function to celebrate the Eighth month of pregnancy was performed in my in-law's family. Babu brought his camera and took several snaps of me with a fat tummy. My daughter Vinodhini was born to me on 23rd May 1993. My sibilings were surprised to see the baby and welcomed the new entrant to the family with great jubilation. Babu wondered at how tiny the parts of a baby could be!

13

The Derogatory Words

During the fourth month, Vinodhini was trying her best to turn over. Whenever she was awake, she would make an attempt to turn over but in vain. Seeing her struggling so much, Babu intervened. Once, when she was attempting to turn over, Babu pushed her the other side and she lay happily on her tummy, lifting up her head and looking around strangely. He liked her so much and admired her tiny parts. From time to time, he would buy her gifts and toys. As she kept growing, Babu presented her with a cradle first, followed by a walker, tricycle and a small chair. Once when he showed her a magic doll, she started crawling towards him curiously. He enjoyed her baby talk and would spend the time playing with her whenever he was at home. Once, when I put her in a cradle, she started screaming. I sat down beside the cradle and started rocking it. Babu also came and sat down near the cradle and started singing a song and immediately she drifted off to sleep. When my maternity leave of four months was over, I decided to leave my daughter under my mother's care and accompanied my husband to my in-law's house. During the weekends, I would join my daughter and spend my time with her.

I stopped giving my income to my mother after marriage. Also, father had spent the whole retirement money for my marriage and my family returned to square one. Father was finding it difficult to run the family. The quarrels over money between my parents continued once again. I started to worry about my father. My sister Usha had to get married and how was father going to conduct her marriage with no money on hand. How much had Usha helped all of us! She had slogged like a bull, and even now was taking care of my baby. Is it not my responsibility to repay her kindness ? I was so disturbed by this fact. I started breaking my head on how best I could be of help to my father.

Whenever I requested my husband for financial help for my family, he would get angry. He would say, "it is a disgrace on the part of your parents to seek help from you, even after getting you married ; for now you belong to another family. " And I would think, it was my father who had undergone so much of hardship in his life to educate me and also accompanied me to several interviews until I settled in this best job. And as luck would have it, my marriage was settled immediately after getting this job and I could be of help to my family only for a short time.

And once, when I apprised him about this fact, he said rather curtly, "your father has afterall just done his duty! By the way, you are not the only daughter in the family. Your father has three sons and it is their responsibility to take care of the family. You don't have to unnecessarily worry about your family !" I pocketed the insult without offering any adverse remarks. I did not wish to justify to him that my father went above the call of duty to turn me into a courageous and independent woman in life. Though I was aware of the fact that there was a little truth in his outburst ; at that point of time, his speech seemed derogatory to me. It hurt me so much and instantaneously I took a drastic decision in my life.

Henceforth, I was not going to spread my palms in front of him for any help to my family.

However, the fact that my hands were tied now and that I could not help my father financially was killing me day after day. No matter what, I had to make my family rich. My sister has to get married and it is also my responsibility to contribute whatever I can.

And while dwelling deeply about this, an idea struck me. Father often kept telling me about his friends whose sons went abroad for a job. They earned a good salary and helped their parents financially. Father regretted that none of his sons succeeded in getting a foreign job and be of support to him financially. However, he hoped that Babu would one day go abroad and make the family rich. Having heard of his desire several times, I was now bent upon fulfilling my father's dream. Perhaps, I could request Babu to look for an overseas job. He would then be able to earn a lot of money and be of help to my family. He could make my family rich. If I succeeded in doing so, I would have still contributed to my family's welfare indirectly. This fact filled me with happiness and I wished to somehow coax Babu and send him abroad. I wanted him to step into my shoes and help the family. I decided to offer prayers to God and seek His blessings so that my brother gets a good job in a foreign country.

One weekend, I discussed about this with Babu. "No way!" was his immediate reply. Further, he said, "I am having the worst experience with all these Overseas Manpower agencies! They demand a huge recruitment fee and where do I go for such huge sums! And I am not willing to spare even a single paise towards this!" This infuriated me and I started yelling at him, "If you refuse to help father, who do you think is going to help him. Being a son, don't you think that it is your responsibility to help your family and get your sister married?" Once again he responded in a harsh way, "I am not going abroad!

Don't keep pestering me !" I was worried about his rigidness, and now I softened a little. "Please Babu, change your mind! Don't be so stubborn. I shall pray for you and see to it that you don't have to shell out a single paise for this purpose! I am confident that my prayers will yield good results! You will get a job abroad and that too without having to pay any sum to the recruiting agencies. Is that O K with you now ?" And Babu assented to this. That week-end I returned home with haughtiness. If my plan met with success, my family would become financially sound and there would be no need for me to request my husband for any financial help! Babu had now agreed to go abroad and he was going to earn more money and make my family rich!

14

Help from a Stranger

Babu now started applying to various overseas agencies in good earnest. I also started to scan the Sunday newspapers and gave him information on overseas advertisements for the post of AC Engineers. He was now busy attending interviews.

Though he earned a meagre salary, Babu was always interested to equip the house with all modern gadgets. On loan basis, he bought home a tape recorder one day. For the first time, all of us enjoyed listening to our own voices in the tape recorder. Once he bought a washing machine and taught Usha how to use the same. He exchanged the black and white television for a colour television. He wished to do something useful for the family rather than spend it for provisions. When father grumbled about his lavish expenditure, he would say that he would not disturb him in any way and would pay the monthly instalments all by himself.

After my prayers for a government job, resulted in success, I realized that there exists some superior power in the universe which is beyond our control. I considered that power as God and belief in that Power, gave me confidence in life. I believed that we can achieve anything in life ; if we place our firm faith in God. So, now, I started praying to God to bless my brother with an overseas job immediately. And I was really astonished when this prayer too was answered very soon!

One fine day, Babu came home very excited. He told me that he had just attended an interview in a Five Star Hotel at Chola Sheraton. One Mr. Narayanan, who was an Indian doctor, settled in Jamaica, West Indies had interviewed him and was much impressed with him. He at once offered him a job in Jamaica as an AC Engineer. He will be getting a salary of Rs. 10,000/- and an yearly bonus of Rs. 75,000/-. Further, his passport, visa and airtickets would all be taken care of by him. While Babu was narrating his story, I was really thrilled and enraptured and transported to a different world. I was really touched by what God has done to me. I felt immense relief and I was so overwhelmed by the fact that a stranger had volunteered to help my brother in a kind-hearted manner.

I thanked God for the fruition of my prayer. My brother would now earn a lot of money and my family would be able to come out of poverty and lead a rich life! More than anything else, the quarrel between my parents would come to an end. The fact that my father was happy, made me feel exhilarated. I took pride in the fact that I was responsible for the same.

In January 1995 Babu got his appointment letter from Jamaica. His boss, Mr. Narayanan, had sent an appointment letter to Babu which all of us took turns in reading.

"This is to inform you that you have been appointed as Refrigeration Engineer to be employed by Spring Gardens Ltd., Jamaica from middle of March 1995. The location of the job is in the western part of Jamaica, West Indies. The salary and the benefits are attractive. However, the lifestyle is rather simple. Our refrigeration trucks, and the maintenance of these vehicles would be somewhat limited. However, we are looking for a person with managerial responsibilities and the technical knowledge of how to handle refrigeration units. The manager's responsibilities would include inventory keeping, shipping of products to USA from Jamaica and managing custom clearance of products coming into Jamaica to our company. The farm is 30 miles from Montego Bay although part of the activity would happen at the Free Zone in Montego Bay which is Seaside Resort in Jamaica."

I read the letter over and over again with a throbbing heart. Very Soon, Babu installed a phone at home with international call booking facility. Quite often, he received instructions from his boss through phone. He was to leave for Jamaica in March 1995 and before that he was to learn car driving and also acquire some knowledge in the field of horticulture. When father pounded him with questions regarding the nature of job he was going to undertake, Babu explained to him in simple terms. "My boss owns a flower company in Jamaica. He has a farm land in Jamaica cultivating flowers. These are transported in coolers to USA for sale. I am joining there as a Refrigeration Engineer and shall be responsible for any faults or repairs of these coolers!"

My daughter turned two years old and she started entertaining all of us by singing rhymes. Babu was often carried away by her mannerisms and felt sad of leaving her. She started calling him, "Babu Mama" and when he was around, she would keep trotting around him calling out his name. Babu's departure was postponed to June 1995. However, During the first week of May, he received a cheque for Rs. 10,000/- from Mr. Narayanan. Babu always liked to spend money for others and he used this money to buy a costly birthday dress for Vinodini. He purchased a silk saree for Usha and some pants and shirts for himself.

While Babu was getting ready to leave for Jamaica, everyone at home was sad about his separation from the family, The most affected was my mother. She kept reminding him that he had to return after two years, no matter what. And father kept telling him that he had to write frequent letters and also advised him to keep only a few good friends. Babu handed over the keys of his motor bike to Ramesh, my youngest brother and told him that he had to take care of his bike properly by cleaning it every day and give it back to him in good condition on his return to India. Just two days, before Babu's parting, mother broke her leg and was admitted in the hospital for a minor fracture. After seeing her in the hospital, Babu left for Jamaica on 22nd June, 1995. The whole family went to Meenambakkam Airport to bid good bye to him. Finally, when it was time for his security check, he came to Vinu and promised her that he would send many beautiful toys for her, once he reached Jamaica. And when my daughter lifted her little hand and told him, "Bye Babu Mama", his eyes welled up with tears and he took leave of us, without turning back.

On 24th morning, Babu rang up. He told us that he reached Jamaica safely, without any problem and that the time then was 8.30 p.m. The time difference between the two countries was fourteen hours.

15

The Unanswered Letters

I was happy that by successfully sending Babu to a foreign country, the financial crisis in my family was taken care of and Usha's marriage would not be a problem. For, father does not have to worry about money with regard to conducting her marriage. The fact that God was fulfilling all my wishes gave me confidence in life to achieve any thing that I intended to do. I had already made a list of proposals to put-forth to God for His blessing and fulfilment. The first in the agenda was to complete the construction of my house in a grand manner and then plan my second child.

Babu had purchased many household gadgets on loan basis and the amount to be paid every month towards this was Rs. 850/- Before leaving to Jamaica, Babu requested father to pay the monthly instalments regularly and he promised to send him money immediately after receiving his salary. Father agreed to do so. On first of July, as soon as he received his pension, father paid the amount of Rs. 850/- and due to this, he started feeling the pinch of money. He was finding it difficult to run the family with his balance pension.

He was very badly in need of money and he looked forward to Babu's phone call to inform him about his financial crisis, which had arisen mainly because of his shelling out a portion of his pension for his loan instalment. Babu never gave him his contact number and so father could not contact him. He kept counting days with the hope that Babu would send him some money.

During the middle of July 1995, a month after Babu left to Jamaica, we received his first letter. The letter was dated 3. 7. 1995 and it took almost twenty days for his letter to reach us. It read as follows :

Its long since I had thought of writing to you. But I thought I had to first settle down before finding time for this. It was really a wonderful experience on the flights. Madras to Bombay and from Bombay to London and from London I had to take another flight to Montego Bay. Since I was a first time traveller, I had to be very careful in each of the airports. The immigration clearance authorities at Bombay, London and Montego Bay conducted an interview and only then I was cleared at each station. The whole experience was something new and I really enjoyed them. The working hours here is 7 a.m. to 4 p.m. Saturdays and Sundays are off. The temperature conditions here are such that no airconditioning is required. The area of work and the place where I stay are both hilly areas. It is very cold and I believe it would take some time for me to get adjusted to the climate. Food is very costly outside the farm house. For example, one tomato costs about 10 J$ (Jamaican dollars). That is Rs. 10 for a tomato. About rupees four hundred has to be spent if lunch and breakfast are to be had outside. Hence, I am forced to prepare my dishes. Although there is a person assisting us in cooking, he is a specialist in Non-vegetarian food and hence I have begun preparing small items like rice, sambhar, coffee, tea, etc. I do believe strongly that I would be able to manage the situation. The telephone calls are very costly over here. Everything is costly in Jamaica. Almost five times *the cost when you compare with India. It is long since I have had the taste of Indian Sambhar and rasam. Here, no body knows of chapati or puri. Only God knows what my future will be like in the coming months. Sometimes, it makes me feel that home is really sweet, a nice place to live, to eat, to quarrel and what not.*

How is Vinodini ? How is my bike ? How is mother's health. What has happened to Usha's marriage ? What has happened to Babu's marriage ? Why don't you find suitable alliance for both and fix them up.

Hemalatha : Kindly pray for me. Pray that I get used to the Jamaican climate, food and way of life etc.

Father read the letter several times. No where, had Babu mentioned about sending money and this upset father very much. He was disappointed about his casual manner of taking things. And, he was worried about how to cope with the mounting expenses in the family. He spoke at length about his financial crisis to my second brother Raghu, who promised to help him by buying provisions every month. In the meanwhile, father decided to write a letter to Babu, apprising him about the acute financial crisis in the family. He informed him in detail about the pending telephone and electricity bills and the difficulty he was facing in running the family. After nearly a month, when he still did not receive any reply from him, he wrote him another letter; followed by a third letter. But there was not any response from him.

16

A Sign of Relief

The construction of my house had just begun at the time Babu left for Jamaica. I was really disheartened by the fact that Babu would not be there for the house warming ceremony. But then I pacified myself that, he was after all going to return after two years and at that time, I could show him around my grand and well furnished house.

Babu had not spoken to us for a long time nor did he keep his promise of writing letters regularly. All of us were so eager to hear some news from him. We were wondering why Babu had not even dropped a letter for the past three months. I was rather concerned if anything untoward had happened to him. Anything could happen in a foreign land! Was he kidnapped by somebody? Did he show his anger to anybody over there and did this result in his imprisonment ? Was he sick and lying in hospital ? Was he trapped somewhere ? Such dreadful thoughts kept racing in my mind quite often. For what other reason could hold him from making a call ? Or atleast write a letter ? Whenever father and I met, we were discussing about Babu and his carelessness in not keeping in touch with the family. One day, father gave me Babu's fax number which he had obtained from a copy of his appointment letter that he had carefully preserved, and requested me to send a letter to him. After sending the fax, I prayed to God and waited in abated breath for his phone call. What if he does not call up ? I suffered from a gut wrenching pain at the thought of this. I felt relieved when Babu called up that night. However, he spoke just for a few seconds only. All that he managed to say was, "the company I have joined in is on strike. I have now shifted to another place! I have written to you in detail!"

Father was in great turmoil on hearing this. This meant that there would be no money from Babu in the near future. He was much perturbed over this. But I heaved a sigh of relief that my brother was safe and nothing adverse had happened to him.

17

The Land of Wood and Water

At last, during the middle of October 1995, we received another letter from Babu. This time his letter was pretty long and he had written the following :

It is really long since I thought of communicating to you all. I should regret that I had lots of problems in getting adjusted to a foreign climate. Before going into further details, I would be failing in my part if I don't thank you all for having come all the way to the airport to see me off. I should especially thank Mr. and Mrs Gnanasekar for being so kind to me. I should admit that if at all I am in an environment of foreigners, i.e. abroad, the credit would go to father and Hemalatha. But for your constant encouragement and support, I should have still been indulging only in fantasies and nothing more. I should thank Hemalatha for her constant prayers.

In the meanwhile, let me tell you something about my country. "Jamaica" means the land of wood and water. The older name for Jamaica was "Xaymaca". This land is a paradise for vacation. This beautiful island was inhabited by Amerindians when Columbus arrived in May 1494 and claimed it for Spain. Later it was claimed for the King of England during 1655. Jamaica remained as a British colony until August 1962. Then it became an independent soverign state.

This island is blessed with lovely weather all year, beautiful white and black sand beaches, green hills and mountains, cool, clear streams and rivers and the people noted for their hospitality and friendly nature. Numerous attractions have been developed for the visitors' relaxation and enjoyment. These include a myriad of water sports, golfing, mountain climbing, horse back riding, cycling and rafting, dancing to the hypnotic rhythms of the island.

"Kingston" is the capital of Jamaica. Traditionally, visitors spend their vacation in the cities of Kingston and Montego Bay, the rural seaside towns of Port Antonio, Ochorios and Negril and the cool Mountain town of Mandeville. "Kingston" is the largest English speaking city in the Caribbean and houses the seat of Government. It is blessed with one of the best natural harbours in the world and offers visitors attractions ranging from beaches to mountain treks. Montego Bay is the second city and the tourist capital of the island. "Ocho rios" is a little fishing village. "Port Antonio" is nestled beneath the blue mountains, "Mandeville" is important for its natural features. "Negril" is twenty miles of the finest white sand beaches in the world.

Well, you should have been bored up reading the history of the country. I realize this. You might be interested in matters related to "Bread and Butter" rather than constitutional matters.

After the final wave at the Madras airport to you all, I had to check-in my luggage and my hand baggage. Since it was a totally new experience, I did not know what I had to do first. But I had a handful of useful information which helped me a lot. My baggage was to be placed at a different passage and I had to pass through a different gate. The security did their work and with the boarding pass in my hand and hundreds of passengers in front of me, I could not imagine that I was going to travel by air. The flight arrived and we were carried in mini buses to the flight.

As I entered into the plane, the air-hostess was seen welcoming everyone and bowing down saying "Welcome to Jet Airways." Although I had the seat number on the boarding pass / ticket, I did not know if mine was the window side or the corner side. I had to confirm this. Fortunately I was on the window side. The flight was ready to take off, there was an announcement stating that the seat belts should be fastened and we were off. It was so nice to see the city from the top. It was just full of lights and as the plane was getting higher, the lights could hardly be visible.

Usha's favourite Sanjay Kapoor, Juhi Chawla and a few other actors were sitting in front of me. After all, they are human beings like us. The airhostess first served each passenger with a towel dipped in water to refresh ourselves. Then came a trolley with closed sachets. I was just wondering on what it could be. I could see the passengers pick two packs, one from each extreme of the plate. I got my share but did not know what it could be. I opened one sachet carefully and found a piece of cotton. I was contemplating on why the hell were they serving cotton. I tried to see what the guy sitting next to me was doing. I could see him cut the piece of cotton into two. He plugged both of his ears with it. I too did this. But after a short while, I wanted to confirm if all the passengers were doing the same. I could hardly see a few. So, I casually removed the plugged cotton and put them into the "Sick-bag". The other sachet was a piece of choclate. We were just being served something or the other. Finally, it ended with dinner.

Reaching "Bombay" in about an hours' time, I had to rush to the international airport. For persons who had booked their tickets with British Airways, a special bus was seen standing outside the airport. I immediately got into it. On reaching the airport, I had to check on all formalities like immigration, security, etc. You would never believe that I never realized getting into the flight. The Airways have set so much of comfort to people. Once you get the boarding pass, you have to clear the immigration. After the immigration formalities, you have duty free shopping complex, then you have to again check the boarding pass along with the passport. I could not believe on how I had entered into the flight after that. I could then analyze that the exit of· the plane was linked to the airport by means of some sophisticated equipments. Hence you could do your shopping before taking your seat. Well, then the "Heathrow Airport" and then the "Gatwick Airport" and finally "Sangster Airport". Let me not bore you people again narrating my experience.

Incidently, I should tell you that the time right now is 6.57 p.m. I am preparing some noodles and tomato soup. The gas cylinder is empty. The spare cylinder is also empty. I have devised a new technique of using the lantern. You should understand that I have become a better cook. I should admit that I don't have any fascination for any non-vegetarian items although the access is so easy. I tried to experiment with a few samples, but I don't feel the taste as great as that of the vegetarian stuff. Well, be happy that I am still belonging to your group of "Saiva Thullava Vellalar, Pure Vegetarian, Orthodox. . . . " I should ask father how his hobby - finding a suitable match for Usha is working. Are you still trying to find someone for the poor girl ? It's a pity. I regret so much for Usha. Dear father, for how long do you wish to give such a harsh treatment to her. Don't you think it is your duty to get her married to someone. Why are you failing so much. What is your problem. Is it the horoscope that is failing so badly or is it your proceedings. I hope to hear something positive very soon.

Still my tomato soup is not ready. I am a bit hungry. But I have decided to complete my writing work before dinner.

Reaching Jamaica, I had a West Indian Manager waiting for me at the airport. I was picked up at the airport and brought to the place where I had to stay. It is called "The cabin" and was owned by the whites earlier.

The time now is 8.20 p.m. I had some noodles. These were sent from the States. Looks like as though I did not fry them properly. Left them in the fridge. Not tasty. Its made out of wheat flour.

I am feeling so drowsy. I have been entangled with another problem. Luckily God has been helping me in sorting out things favourable to me. I have a lot of plans and I do hope I would see the fruits of my dreams. Hope you all pray for me. I shall discuss my problems that I had from day one in my next letter. I shall also write to you about my future plans. You don't have to worry about me. My experience, confidence and the Lord's blessing have always been grateful to me. I should thank father who had trained me in such a way. But for the way in which he had brought me up, I could have failed in many of my dealings. He had always encouraged me in doing things I felt were right. He had given me so much of freedom and this really has enabled me in learning more.

Let me take a quick glance at your previous letters :

Your letters dated 17.7.1995, 28.8.1995 and 11.9.1995. You had mentioned it had taken only 10 days for my letter to reach you. Probably it was because it was posted from the States. Letters sent from Jamaica would take about 20 days.

Please don't expect letters on a regular basis. I have so many other things to do. I assure you that if there is any serious problem / emergency, I would surely inform you.

Nice to hear all are okay over there.

Nice to hear the bandage on mother's foot is off. It is also good that Hemalatha and Gnanasekar have a good touch with the family.

My health : I am not a kid and please don't worry yourself.

Sorry, I am very drowsy. I don't get words to further proceed. Well, "Home is always sweet" and I miss each and every one of you. But "To sacrifice short term benefits would see you achieve your long term goals". I believe that and hope its all for the betterment.

I really wonder how Usha manages the cooking. As I am practically doing the cooking work here, I realize how tedious the process is. I am missing Vinu so much. The word "Babu mama" always lingers in my ears.

Mother and Father : How are fights over money ? Hope I could help you in solving the financial problem very shortly. Please be patient. I do remember the debts you have. I don't find any time to concentrate on "money transfers". Well, I would like to make myself mentally free and once I feel I am okay, I shall start sending a few dollars to you.

The time is about 9.00 p.m. and I would fall asleep soon. So, let me say good night to you all, before I finish my letter.

Note : Confirm the condition of Hero Honda bike to me. If the vehicle is not used, atleast start the vehicle daily, raise the engine and shut off. This would ensure that the vehicle is in good condition. How are you managing the Rs. 890 per month for the bank ?

I was rather relieved to see Babu's letter after a long time and commenced reading the same avidly. I felt glad that Babu had thanked me for the encouragement I gave him and for all my efforts to send him abroad. Also, he had finally realized the importance of prayers and I felt happy that he would henceforth not grumble over my spending too much time on that.

Babu had patiently written about the historical data of Jamaica. The description of the natural beauty of Jamaica lured me at once and I longed to be there in the midst of the green and lush trees, the hills and seas. I considered Babu to be really lucky for God had blessed him with a job in such a peaceful country.

I appreciated the fact that Babu had so quickly got acquainted with the names of the villages, towns, hills and beaches of Jamaica. His recount of his first time flight experience was interesting. But his mention about the various attractions that Jamaica offers to its visitors assailed my mind with doubts. Jamaica is actually a tourist spot. The cost of living in a tourist country would surely be high and Babu had to shell out a lot of money for his food, clothing and shelter. This being the circumstance, how was he going to save money, if any, and send it to father.

Father, however, was not delighted about whatever Babu had written. He did not get carried away by Babu's appreciation of him in giving him freedom. Nor did he get dejected when Babu had belittled him for not having found a suitable match for Usha so far. But what distressed him most was the fact that Babu had not mentioned anything about sending money to him. He was already turning mad due to paucity of funds. Father voiced his concern over this to me. "What exactly is he doing there ? How can he be so irresponsible ? Has he forgotten his family at No. 2, Gandhi Street, which he had left in dire poverty before leaving to Jamaica?" I tried to assuage his fears and reassured him, "probably, he has not yet got settled over there. Or may be he is not having time! He has after all informed that once he is mentally free, he would think about money transfer! It is just a matter of time!"

Though I had allayed father's fears, my mind was plugged with several questions. He had referred to some problems which he had bravely and confidently confronted with ; which he would be narrating in his next letter. What exactly was he talking about? I was anxious to read his next letter.

18

Home Sweet Home

One evening my mother called up. She seemed to be in a very depressed mood and when I asked her if anything was wrong, she immediately told me the cause of her worry. "Another storm has hit our family!", she began. "It is all due to your brother Raghu! This morning, two sturdy men had come to our house asking for him. They divulged the fact that Raghu had used his credit cards and had purchased things for Rs. 35,000/-. If their dues are not settled at once, they would even take the drastic step of arresting him. I then told them that it would not be possible for us to arrange for such a huge sum at a short notice but however them that we would give Rs. 10,000/- within the next two days! After much pleading, they finally consented!" Before I could even recover from the daunting news, mother continued, "I now have no body else whom I can ask for help except you! Please talk to your husband and arrange to give me a loan of Rs. 10,000/-. I shall return the same to you once Babu sends some money!" Her voice grew shaky and she started to cry. Promising her that I will try my best, I placed the receiver on the cradle, wondering whether I would be able to succeed in persuading my husband to help me.

When mother told about this to Raghu, he had taken the whole issue rather lightly and said, "why the hell are they talking to you ? Ask them to contact me and I will answer them!" Provoked by his cool manner of taking things, father shouted at him, "the men who had come today were serious about taking you to task, for not paying up the dues. They would go to any extent and I warn you to be careful with them. It is you who have to go and meet them and explain our predicament to them. By the way, what did you buy for Rs. 35,000/- using your cards?" Raghu was quick to respond, "it is for your family that I have been spending all the money. Babu has not sent a single pie so far and you were completely dependent on me. I had in fact agreed to buy the monthly provisions, but unfortunately, my salary was held up due to the financial crisis in our company, which is at the verge of closing down shortly. I was forced to use the credit card and with no salary, I could not even pay the minimum amount due. Very soon, I may lose my job and I am in a tension as to what to do next!"

That night, I talked to my husband about this and as usual he berated my family and refused to offer any help. "By helping them, from time to time, you would be making your people lethargic and careless in life! They would take everything for granted and keep depending on you for any exigencies! Don't encourage this! Nip it in the bud itself, though it may bring bad name to you!" But I was in no mood to listen to him. How can he refuse to help me, even after promising him that I would repay his loan! It was my family's reputation that was at stake, and if I do not help them at the hour of need, who else will! was not prepared to let him have his way! I kept harrying him for money, justifying to him that it was a loan I was asking him and that I would repay the amount once my brother Babu sent some money. Finally, unable to bear my importunity, he went to the ATM centre and withdrew the money and gave it to me.

I, in turn handed over the money to father and told him point blank, "my husband has drawn this money from a ATM centre and please arrange to repay the amount at the earliest to avoid any misunderstanding between us!" Father understood my plight, and after vowing to me that he would return the same within a month, he immediately wrote a firm letter to Babu, requesting him for urgent financial help.

Father waited eagerly for a reply from Babu to his letter. The letter finally arrived during the fag end of December 1995, nearly six months after his going to Jamaica. In a very dejected mood, father gave me the letter to read. And I grabbed it from his hand and started to read the same inquisitively.

Hope this letter of mine finds you in good health and high spirits. I am quite okay! Received your letter. You people are very much interested in my writing letters. But you don't know that I am also interested in writing so much to you. But why don't you wait for a couple of months till I settle down. Once things are smooth, I would assure you of atleast one letter a week. Till such time, bear with me.

I do regret that I have been unable to support you in any way for the past five months. But with the Lord's blessings, I should say I would compromise for the above, rather I would compensate doubly very shortly.

Although I wound not be writing to you in detail, I would like to brief you with the recent happenings.

Well, I am not working for Mr. Narayanan anymore. I have been relieved from the company. However, I have his housing facility still in my possession.

You would be surprised to know that I am a Director-Engineering in a firm. I am also a shareholder of the company. We are dealing with Refrigeration and Airconditioning, also *home appliances. I would be writing to you about this exclusively in my next letter. But pray God that my new endeavour would be a success. Very shortly, I shall give you my new address. I would be getting my telephone connection in my new premises in a few months. Once I get this facility, we won't have problem with regard to communication. We could keep in touch regularly. I think you are aware that the charges to India from Jamaica is about 70 J$ per minute.*

It was with great difficulty that I could get relieved. I have already filed a legal suit but asked my lawyer to keep the case pending. Once I see the old guy Narayanan wagging his tail again to me, I would swear, God willing, I shall claim a heavy compensation for whatever good things he had done to me. Please don't worry yourselves with the silly things going around me. I am educated, reasonably good in communication, self-confident and highly motivated. Lastly but not the least is, God's favour and your prayers. Hence, you don't have to bother about me in any way. Very shortly, I would make the old guy realise all his mistakes and he would surely regret for all his wrong doings.

Okay. Having told you about myself, let me tell you something interesting about this country. If you have the world map in front of you and try to locate Jamaica, you would be finding it difficult. Why ? Because, it is just a dot that indicates Jamaica i. e (.). But you would not believe that this country is a paradise spot for the honeymooners, holiday / vacation enjoyers from the States and United Kingdom. This is a tiny island. Let me describe to you the country precisely.

Well, I would classify the country into two depending upon the people (1) Rural / village (2) Urban / town.

The rural area : People are illiterate. Their language is "Batwa" (I would tell you that its broken English) For e.g.,
In Batwa : Me A Come

In English : I am coming

In Batwa : Me A Go

In English : I am going

In Batwa : Wha ?

In English : What ?

I am already crazy with the foreign accent. Well I have become adjusted to this language. The funny thing is, I have been to almost all parts of this country. But I find the people asking me, "How is that you speak so good English ? Which country are you from ? We have not seen any foreigner speak such good English"

Well, I should not boast about this. Because the credit goes to father and his strong foundation. I mean the basics were strong. You would not believe that I no longer feel like a stranger in this foreign land. All that makes me strange is :

(1) One Tomato - 15 J$

(2) One Brinjal - 20 J$

(3) One ladies finger - 3 J$

(4) Cabbage - 50 J$

(5) One onion - 5 J$

(6) One carrot - 8 J$

(7) One handful of peas - 20 J$

Well, It should really sound funny to you all. But you know "It is all in the game".

You know something. I have started buying tinned vegetables. It is a mixture of all vegetables in a tin. This is economical. It is cooked and hence can be had direct. You know what I do, I heat them and have it all with rice and peas. So nice. But it is a long time since I have had the food served to me. You know what, Usha used to bring the cooked items into the hall. I never even brushed my teeth. I sat down with the big round plate with Purial , kootu and then rice. I left the purial, kootu and added sambar into the food. Oh! The aroma and the flavour! I would have,

Sambar..Sambar..Sambar..Rasam..Curd

I don't know when I would taste them again in the above sequence.

Well, I have so much to write that I am getting confused. I was telling you about the rural area. The villagers live out of farming. They plant their own crops. You have a couple of schools, couple of churches. In the rural area, there is only one bus in the early morning and one in the late evening. The rural area is mostly among the hills. i.e. about 4000 ft above the sea level. You would find only one house in a circumference of about 50 meters. You could imagine for yourself on how the area would be. Its only greenery you could see wherever you go. Hills and hills, serpentine roads. Well, how do I express it to you. If any one of you is a lover of nature, you would know.

The Jamaicans are lovers of music. They love music more than their food. They hardly have a bath but their body and clothes always have a good perfumed smell. Most of the Jamaicans don't smoke. They drink wine. Their food is very simple. Bread, eggs, chicken and Yam is their daily food for week days. On the weekends, rice and peas are cooked. "Rice and Peas" is the most popular and commonly used food in restaurants, fast foods. . . . The dress they wear, my goodness do you want to know. . . . . . It is mostly a three piece. Don't ask me anything more. Its so awful that I am losing interest in getting married.

Well, talking about the marriage in western culture. Let me be serious. You should not ask anyone in the western world if he / she is married. But I have discovered a way :

(1) How is your boy friend ?
(2) How many kids you have ?
(3) How do you manage ?
(4) How many boy friends do you have ?
(5) Are you married to any one of them ?

No. . . . No. . . No. . . . No. . . . . .

You talk to about 10 women, (eight would say "No")

The Western Culture is "His children, Her children and our children"

No body thinks of marriage, because they don't know what it is. I mean it. It is so funny to look at school girls going to school with their baby. It is more funny to see them walk on the streets with their bulging bellys. . . . . Chi. . . . . I am so shy. . . . . . . I don't want to say more about this culture.

One thing I should confirm "Home is always sweet home, India is India and cannot be compared with this country. "

Well, the urban way of living is very easy for you to contemplate. The bigger ones, the smaller ones, the shorter ones, the longer ones. . . . . all busy. Cars busy on the road, restaurants busy, business centres busy, nothing to say.

In the meantime, let me tell you that I had a very good and great deal of time (a couple of months) working in the airport of Jamaica. It was really an interesting experience seeing the planes landing and taking off. It is more interesting to watch the helicopters and smaller planes.

Now that I have become a shareholder and director of a company I have the privilege of recruiting candidates. But this is not the right time for Raghu to think of all these. He has to wait till Usha's marriage is completed and our house extended. Once this is over, I would contemplate on this.

Regarding my bike, I understand Raghu wanted to replace the front shock absorbers. But let him check if it can be serviced. The absorbers could be serviced. If not, let him replace it. But still this is not a major problem, except you will have to slow down when you approach pot holes.

How is mother's health ? I do hope "Athipathi Nursing Home" is the right medicare unit for her. In case of any serious problems, I think Raghu should have access to Apollo Hospital or elsewhere, where you would have better treatment.

Hope Hemalatha and Gnanasekar are doing well. How far have they reached with the construction work ?

I was really surprised on how father could equate Baba and Babu. Well, He had written on. . . . . And stated, I don't know when and how BAB(U)A is going to bless. . . . .

I could not stop laughing, but still I know how serious he was or rather he meant it.

God willing, let me hope to transfer some currency by the end of March 1996. Although I cannot assure you, how much or when exactly. It should be a reasonable amount.

Well, Before I end my letter, you may want to know what I am doing right now. I am preparing some snacks. You know what. Its "DASHIN" (a sweet root / vegetable) and some tea. The time is about 3. 00 p. m Looks like as though I have some pain at the left of my neck since I had been leaning for a very long time. No "Iodex", No "Zandubalm". You have something known as "Rubbing Alcohol"

Yes, I ask my guy, West Indian, "Yeoh, you know wha hapn, me neck severe and bad pain. Wha medicine you have. "

"No Sam, No medicine" comes the reply. "Me a have but sommonne pick off"

My goodness. No medicine. Let me try my yoga exercises. Oh, I feel some burning smell. Looks like my food is ready to be had. Okay let me enjoy my food while you enjoy yours.

Like father, I had also been anxiously waiting for Babu's letter ; expecting some good news that he was going to send some money. But when the letter came through, it took but a moment to dash the hopes I had held for so many days. My mind was filled with several questions for which I could find no answers. Why did he leave his job with Mr. Narayanan ? He was in a foreign land, and did he not know how to behave in a foreign land where everything is so unfamiliar. Once again, he had lost his temper! His temper was not only ruining his life but ours too. With no job, how was he ever going to be of help to us ? This letter also left me with a doubt as to whether he had actually read our last letter or not ; for there was no mention in it about his offering immediate monetary help to us. He had promised to send money only during March next year and this being the case, how was father going to repay the loan to my husband ? I lost my peaceful sleep!

19

Another Bombshell

"Since you are working in a big organisation and earning a good salary, your family members think that you are bound to help them at the time of crisis!" My husband rebuked me one evening just as he stepped into the house. I could not make out head or tail of what he was telling. Was he referring to my promise I made to him that I would be repaying his loan as soon as we receive some money from Babu ? I asked him to be a little clear and then he let the cat out of the bag. "Your brother Raghu came to my office today. He told me that since the bank people are sitting on his head, he required an urgent loan of Rs. 25,000/- and I had borrowed it from one of my friends and helped him!" Another bombshell on my head! How was I ever going to cope up with that ? One flaw in my husband's character was that he was weak to flattery. If any one spoke so high of him and begged him to do some thing, he would easily give in. "Why did you help him, without even informing me?" I screamed at him.

"He told me that Babu would be sending some money during March this year and that he would repay the whole loan he has taken from me! By the way, won't you make my life miserable if I refuse to help your family ? Stop putting on an act in front of me!" My husband was after all right. I simply pocketed the insult without retorting him.

The new year 1996 had begun in good earnest. All of us were looking forward to the month of March, as Babu had promised to send some money during this time.

However, I was really pained by the fact as to why Babu had discontinued his job with Mr. Narayanan. I was wondering what exactly was he doing now ? How was he leading his day to day life, with no job on hand ? To get all my doubts cleared, I wrote a letter to Babu asking him to explain everything in detail. I wished to know the reasons for his severing his ties with Mr. Narayanan. Further, I also advised him that if things were not smooth in Jamaica, he could very well return to India any time and continue having his favourite food ; of which he was so fond of.

Very soon, we received his letter dated 8. 1. 1996 :

Hope this letter of mine finds you in good health & high spirits. Well, I should apologize for not writing letters frequently. But you should try to understand my position. I have just been relieved of my duties from Narayanan's company. As I wrote to you earlier my new address for communication would be as above. You would be aware that I am a Director and Shareholder of a company that does not mean a big benefit. Raghu would be able to understand and explain to you all, what "Shareholder & Director" means. This would be the dividend or profits shared on a fixed term. However, since I have been relieved from the wretched company of Narayanan, I am mentally free and happy. Shortly, I believe things would turn around. Till such time, I don't want you to build any high ambitions about me. Please don't expect me to write to you on a regular basis nor expect anything else from me till I settle down. The new company of mine gets me fully involved in meeting people and exploring market opportunities for the business to widen. Hence, you would surely understand how difficult the task would be. Kindly pray that the new endeavour of mine would turn out to be a success.

By God's grace, I believe that the beginning of March would surely see things getting better. Hopefully, I could contribute something to you all.

Home had always been sweet. I really miss each one of you. I miss the good food I used to have - SAMBHAR / RASAM / CURD. (In the big plate with porial & kootu), I remember getting up from bed, gargling my mouth and having belly full. Well, I understand that's how life is. "Man proposes and God disposes", this has so much of meaning. But each failure builds up more confidence in one's career and more faith in God. I have also understood that the only solution to our problems is "PRAYER".

Well, I should not bore you people with godly affairs. Anyhow, I miss the Christmas sweets and the Deewali sweets. You would be interested to know how the Jamaicans celebrate their Christmas and New Year. "All the Bars are packed, the roads are all busy. People are so busy that you find the hospitals / clinics filled with teenage school going / college going girls testing themselves for pregnancy tests during April". Well, this is how it goes. The young and old men can all be seen with their girl friends. They call this the so called "Christmas spirit". Thank goodness, that I did not have an opportunity to get into this Christmas spirit.

Well, how are things progressing at home ? How well are the plans for Usha's marriage going on ? It is really unfortunate that I would not be able to participate fully in it. Fortunately, there is a good team, Raghu, Gnanasekar and Ramesh with an energetic leader - Mr. Sivadoss (my father) to lead the function in a prosperous way. I pray that I should atleast help you financially. I hope I would.

I don't think I was in a good mood while starting this letter and hence you may not find it very interesting. I am just thinking on what I should write but unable to flash the thoughts on to the paper. Well, let me write some thing about the Jamaican climate.

The climate is called as the "tropical climate". You have only three types of climate - cold, colder and coldest. Although you may find a few towns hot. The rain water is the only means of water for all purpose. (with the exception of cleaning their buttocks) People shit and use tissue/toilet papers. But, I continue to use water for that purpose. Sounds very awful.

Well, the way in which the water is collected is interesting. All the houses are constructed in such a way that the water from the slopes gets drained to the sump/tank. 90 per cent of the houses are made up of only wood. The floor, the walls and the roof even the shelves, etc. It is believed that bricks are costly. Since the whole country is an endless expanse of trees, wood is lesser in cost. It looks like as though I have stayed in Jamaica for a very long time. I would like to venture into other Caribbean countries like Cuba, Trinidad, Botswana. . . . . Well, I would love to go to the States. It is hardly an hour's journey from Jamaica. But I will have to arrange the Visa and find the vitamin "Pa" (paisa) (probably from God) and then plan for the trip. Till such time, I should be happy with this tiny island. The desire of going to the States becomes more intense, when I see the visitors to my country. (Note, Jamaica has become my country now). It is really so nice to see the whites. I really wonder on how they could be so colourful. It is like as though their body is fully painted with pink colour. The females are like mannequins. So lovely to look. Especially with their two piece dress on the beaches. Don't ask me if I spend most of the time on the beaches. Well, when you are on the roads, you cannot stop watching these ; the beaches are along the roads mostly.

What else do I write ? No way of getting further. . . . . Yes, let me tell you something about my hair. "YOUAHAIR AM PRETTY MAAN, LOVELY YOU HAIR!" I reminicize the days when father used to compel me in getting the hair cut. I have started having funk or what ever you name it. 99 % of the people here are with curly hair. Whenever I go to get my hair cut, the barber hesitates saying, do you want to cut your lovely hair ? Well, so it goes.

Here are a few interesting facts :

Western Culture : To brush their teeth before going to bed only because water is very precious - don't waste them - that is why they don't wash their buttocks and use tissue paper / toilet papers for this purpose.

Smile Wholeheartedly : "No bathing Sir, only towel bath. Do bathing in the seas. Don't find time, use perfume instead.

Don't laugh, I mean it : Want to get a hair cut, you have to pay 200 J$ + tax

Want to buy a pair of shoes, you have to pay 2000 J$ and goes up to 10000 J$ + tax

Not for you : One glass of beer 38 J$ + tax

Cost of medication with prescribed tablets : 1000 J$ + tax

One audio casette : 400 J$ + tax

Funny Jamaican saying : "The lord had come to earth and seen me working. He was so impressed with my work. But when he looked at my salary, he wept bitterly and went back to heaven. "

"HOME SWEET HOME" : But I plan to stay in Jamaica for atleast five years. Once, I start making money (I mean saving money), I would love to visit India, at least once in a year.

Cost of one tomato, is 20 J$. Price of everything is going up. Cost of one motor bike is Rs. 1,30,000/-) So, please take care of my bike properly. Lubricate the chains and keep the vehicle tidy. Use the vehicle at least once weekly. Or start the bike and raise the throttle and shut it off. This would ensure the vehicle is in good condition. Do this daily in the morning for one minute.

I was not inspired by his elevation to the position of Director of a company he has started on his own with a Jamaican partner. From the facts enumerated by him in a casual manner, few things became apparent to me. There was going to be no money from him in the offing. Probably, he was taking all father's letters requesting for money, as a mere joke!

However, one thing was crystal clear to me! I had been unnecessarily worrying about his leaving the job of Mr. Narayanan. Now that fear has gone! He was changing over into a tough and courageous guy ; bubbling with self-confidence and ready to face any situation in life!

20

A Good News and a Bad News

Babu had enquired in his previous letter as to how the things were progressing at home. Father had been burning the midnight lamps, from time to time, apprising him in an elaborate manner about the developments in the family. And if he had read those letters meticulously, he would have pretty well known that things were in fact regressing, back at home.

One evening Raghu came home very excitedly. He informed us that he had a bad news and a good news for all of us. The bad news was that he had lost his job. Even before we could recover from the shock, he came out with the good news ; which was even more appalling. He told us that, he intended to start a new business of his own. He was planning to buy a second hand ambassador car and give it to a travel agency. Father was against this and immediately protested, "this is a business fit for the uneducated people. With your B. Com. degree, you could do something better!" But Raghu was very enthusiastic about his new venture and he said, "I had already arranged for a loan of Rs. 1. 65 lakhs and the car is coming home this week end!" Father expressed his fears to Raghu but it only fell on deaf ears. He convinced him by telling, that the travel agency had promised to pay him Rs. 10,000/- every month and the amount he had to pay to the pawn broker every month was only Rs. 6,000/-. After a year, the car would become his and he would be able to make even more profit with it. Further he said, "what is to be done ? There is no money from Babu so far and with no job, how do you expect me to buy provisions every month ? Moreover, I have already taken loans from all around and how would I be able to repay the same without any income at all?" We were all dumbstruck at his quirky idea. However, we were anxious to see the new car ; while father was eagerly waiting for any news from Babu regarding his promised financial help.

Suddenly, one Saturday morning, when the postman handed over another letter from Babu - this time within a period of a fortnight - we were all astonished. Has he got settled in life? Has he got a lot of spare time? Which is why he was able to think of home and family? With these thoughts running in my mind, I started reading his letter :

Hope this letter of mine finds you in good health and high spirits. I was feeling very bored with nothing much to do. Being fed up with the video and audio programmes, I was just wondering on what I should do. I just thought I should do something productive. Then I realized I could write to you all. Every Saturdays on radio, we have the Indian programmes (6.00 p.m. to 6.45 p.m.). There is also an Indian club in the country. I am yet to become a member of it because it is about 100 miles away from the place I live. I believe you have Indian programmes, such as movies. . . . . & other entertainment. Along with the show, I believe Indian food is also served. From yesterday's news on radio, I understand "BOMBAY" would be screened on February 18th. I am sure I would love to become a member since I am missing some of the nice Indian dishes. By the way, how far have you reached in finalising Usha's marriage. I have not received any letter from you for almost a month.

I do not have much to tell you about myself. I am quite happy that with great difficulty, I got myself relieved from Narayanan's company. I am sure he will find a place in hell (in one of the hot boiling ovens). I don't understand how God favours people like him. Anyhow, I should thank him that he has relieved me and also for having bought me over here. (Note, bought me and not brought me). Well, he thought he could play funny with me. But with God's blessings I had turned it the other way round. I am presently seeking for a job although I work for a company as a Director. The company is new and the salary is based on the profits. Hence, it is obvious that I should have a job right now. Once the business picks up, I may decide on how to progress from then on. But with the Lord's blessings, I hope things would change around shortly.

Here in Jamaica, the cost of living is so much that you can hardly think of "saving". No,. . . . Not even "shaving". You will have to spend about 100 J$ (hundred dollors) for it. Just imagine, you walk out from the super market with a tiny hand bag/plastic cover with the minimum needs of yours, but still realize that you have spent more than 1000 J$. That is the reason why so many Jamaicans try to enter the "STATES". Just consider this : 1 US dollar = 40 J$ (one US dollar is equal to 40 J$) The Jamaican dollar is dropping down day by day, due to which the price of commodities are going up. Well, that's a constitutional problem, you and I are not going to be interested. Nor am I interested in completing this letter and posting it tomorrow. You know I am so moody. You will surely understand by the time you complete reading the entire letter. Because I would stop today and I really don't know when I would continue. Might be because, I had a heavy lunch. Anyhow, I would continue later and not now. . . . .

My Goodness, it has almost taken three weeks to get back to this letter. The weeks were really busy, we had got a big contract. Any how before going further, I wanted to tell you something. In one of the newspapers I came across the following prayer. This prayer has to be said nine times a day. By the ninth day, your prayer will be answered and this has never been known to fail.

"MAY THE SACRED HEART OF JESUS BE ADORED, GLORIFIED, LOVED AND PRESERVED THROUGHOUT THE WORLD NOW AND FOR EVER.

SACRED HEART OF JESUS PRAY FOR US.

SAINT JUDE WORKER OF MIRACLES, PRAY FOR US.

SAINT JUDE HELP OF THE HOPELESS PRAY FOR US. "

(Say this prayer 9 times a day. On the 9th day, or before, it would be answered as it has never failed.) But you will have to publize this after your prayer has been answered.

Why don't you try this prayer. Once your prayer is answered, Raghu can type the prayer, take a few copies of it and distribute to his friends.

You know something, I tried this and only after I started did I realize there was real meaning in it. I got a big contract and also am expecting a job in the company close to my residence. (To be continued in the next letter).

After reading his letter, I realized that Babu had also turned as quirky as Raghu. He was interested more in the self and wished to become a member of an Indian Club. He was losing the control of his mind. Was the Jamaican climate transforming him ? He could not focus wholeheartedly and write a letter to us at a single stretch. He had got interested in a different religion! He was so far away from home - in a totally different world - and for the first time I began to doubt whether this had an impact on his mind too ; which was slowly withdrawing from us ?

21

A Total Fiasco

The car business, which was started in good earnest by Raghu turned out to be a total fiasco. First thing, Raghu did not know how to drive the car and hence had to engage a driver for this purpose. Besides, being a second hand car, it was frequently breaking down. Whatever money he was earning out of this car, he kept spending it on repairs. In order to pay the monthly dues to the pawn broker, Raghu kept borrowing from one source or the other. Ultimately, when he could not keep up his promise of repaying the loans in time, people stopped helping him. Thus the car loan amount, instead of depreciating in value, kept increasing month after month. The damage had already been done !

At last, the much awaited month of March arrived. The fact that we were heading for a bleak future did not deter anyone in the family. For they believed that Babu's money which was forthcoming this month would resolve the financial crisis in the family. Father warned me to keep all matters relating to Raghu a secret and not mention anything about his loss of job or about his car business to Babu and I meekly obliged.

When we received a letter dated 21. 3. 1996 from Babu, I read it with an urgency ; expecting to find some news about his sending money :

I received your letter dated 28. 2. 1996 just an hour before. I should confirm that I have not received your letter dated 13. 1. 1996 (with the photos you had sent). I really don't understand how you could ask me to write without seeing the letter. I understand that there could be delay and a few letters take a couple of months to reach Jamaica. However, I understand you have written something important. Why don't you write to me again regarding those matters. Please note that you will have to write to the above address only. I don't really understnad what financial matters you are facing.

The ridiculous thing is that I don't understand what's happening there and you don't know what's happening here. I mean neither of us know the problems each are facing. Well, from your letter, I understand the following (i.e) you want me to clarify a few things and I am hereby giving you the details :

(1) You have received my letter dated 21. 1. 1996 and 5. 2. 1996 and were not happy. Even I am not happy obviously but you should understand I am trying to do my best to come out of my situation.

(2) Regarding continuity of letters , I mean replying to your letter, I am afraid I really don't have time to concentrate nor reply based on your letter. Because when I finish reading your letter, it goes into the file and that's it. When I am in a relaxed mood, I write to you but don't check with the file.

(3) Yes, I already mentioned to you earlier that I got your telegram. But you really don't understand why I don't call you. The reason is very simple. You know I am presently staying in a different Parish (after I had been relieved from Narayan's company). Now, this Parish / State

presently is not linked up with the telephones. Any how I will surely try to find a solution to this problem. I will soon try to contact you through phone.

(4) *Regarding letters to be written regularly, you know I am really trying hard to write to you atleast once a week. Okay let me make a commitment to you all. On every Sunday, I plan to write to you, beginning April 1996. I think you would be happy now.*

(5) *Regarding the new company, I am the Director, Manager and Engineer. I get my pay. Why do you people worry. I have saved about J$ 40,000 dollars. I really don't understand why you should worry about my day to day or monthly expenditure. Well, the arrangement made is temporary and I would be trying my best to get into the capital of this country. So that things turn around good for you and me. I am trying my best to transfer a bulk amount to your account in the bank. When I transfer the money, I would inform you through telephone. But this is not the right time. You know why ? I really don't have any security and don't want to take any risk by transfering the money that I have right now. By God's grace, I have been healthy till date. Just imagine if something goes wrong. You know the consultation charges a doctor claims - 2000 J$. Just imagine the tests, the medicine etc. . . . No, I don't want to get sick. Thank God that I am as fit as when I had left India.*

(6) *Regarding my recent photo, I really don't know if I can afford the time for it. My main concentration is making money, money and money alone. Well, I will have to plan when I could send it to you. Anyhow, the only change is that I have a beard and a moustache (looks good people say). I have become slim, although I maintain my weight at 65 kg - 70 kg. Regarding the photos you had sent, I regret I have not seen them as yet.*

(7) *Regarding Usha's marriage, I know you would succeed very soon. I would like to hear from you that you have finished her betrothal and fixed a date for her marriage. God willing, I really would wish to be there on those occassions. I really don't know. Any how, lets hope for good things to happen. I won't/don't want to make a commitment.*

(8) *Regarding Usha's graduation, I think she is eligible to enter the "Guiniess Book of World Records". No, I was just teasing. Congratulations! Now its time for her to get a job. I think the best thing to do is to arrange for a full time maid and allow Usha to find a good job.*

(9) *Your financial positions can wait for now. I am not ready as yet. Let me not tell you my plans now. When I tell them to you, I always fail. I will call you when I am sending money to you.*

(10) *Good to hear Vinu would be going to school. I realised she had learnt to write. I saw her sign a letter sent to me by Hema.*

(11) *Good to hear mother is okay and having regular checkups.*

(12) *Nice to hear Raghu is going to office and Hema and Gnanasekar are visiting you every weekend. It is also a pleasure to know that Hemalatha has almost finished the construction of her own home. Congratulations Hema and Gnanasekar.*

(13) *Regarding my marriage, I really don't know what to say. Looks like I am not for it, for now. I have not settled. Things have not settled. I think we can discuss the matter after Usha's marriage.*

(14) Regarding Narayanan, its a long story. I will address the entire matter shortly. Hema had written to me asking for the details. I will have to write a letter separately regarding the issue. Any how I have been relieved from him and in any case if he tries to create any problem to me, he would be in a bad position.

(15) Nature of job now and forever will always be technical and engineering and nothing more. This was the main reason why I fought with that bastard Narayanan and came out. You do know I am short tempered. Nobody could play any kind of tricks with me. Any how that's a different story. I would write to you shortly but I don't think I can make it in one stretch. It would come to you like Part 1, Part 2. . . . . . It would be in a form of a story where the main characters are myself and that wretched guy.

(16) Regarding my decision making, I think I am always in the right direction. I had written to you about my plans to go to the States or migrate to Canada. As on date, these plans are kept in abeyance.

Well, that's it for now. You know something. The postal department is now raising its charges. . . .Guess by how much ? By 100 %. Cost of living is rising day by day. Very hard to save and shave. Any how "HOME SWEET HOME", missing the big plate, porial, kootu, sambhar, rasam and curd and Vinu calling me Babu mama.

ME A WRITE TE YOU NEXT LETTER, SOON TILL THEN BYE.

As I folded the letter, I smiled to myself. Babu had promised to phone up shortly regarding sending money to us and it gave me some hope! And whenever the phone buzzed, I would wish that the chiming sound should linger on. For that meant an international call from Babu!

22

Let Down by the Helpful Stranger

The expected phone call never came. It was already April. The days kept passing by. Raghu was unable to pay the monthly instalment of his car loan. On the other hand, friends and relatives who had helped Raghu by giving him loans were after him. The pawn broker was coercing him to pay up the monthly dues. The pressure of all this was felt by father and he was in turn, diverting his tensions to me. I started worrying about Babu ; as to what exactly was happening to him and why he was unable to keep his promises! Very soon, all my doubts were cleared through a letter we received from Babu, during the end of April :

Hope things are okay. Well, this letter is a description of why I had left Narayanan, the bastard.

Although I had written to you that I would be narrating the entire story in parts and in a story form, I regret I would not be able to do that as I am fully occupied and lack enough time to concentrate. Hence, I would be giving you an overall picture of what exactly took place.

Well, you pretty good know that I was selected as a Refrigeration Engineer in India by the so called bastard. You should have seen the appointment letters and other relevant letters. Now, when I reached Jamaica, on the very first day, I was shocked. I got a different contract paper to sign. The papers told that I was a "Foliage Manager" and the work was in a farm. You would be surprised if I narrate the location of the farm. Its about 2000 ft above the sea level. Temperatures vary between cold, colder and coldest. The houses are fully made of wood and are called as cabins or cottages. One house in a circumference of about 100 meters. The area is very thinly populated. Once in a week / Thursday you would have to drive about 45 miles to the town to buy your daily needs. It takes about 3 hours up and 3 hours down. Six hours on the hilly road. If you make a mistake in your driving, you may not be able to regret it. I hope you understand.

Now, I was really happy with everything except my work. Well I would term myself as a "Farmer" rather than a "Foliage Manager". You all know about me. I am short tempered and cannot take such things easily. No matter what the outcome would be, I fear no challenge, because I have confidence in myself. I just picked up the telephone and called the office in the United States. I asked what the hell was going on. The papers that I got in India were different from the papers you sent to me in Jamaica. You call those as contract agreement. . . . . (yes, the real fight started here)

Dear Narayanan, my foot I care for your contract papers. I swear I would not be in a position to sign the contract papers. Even a mad person would not do it. You had called me to work as an Engineer and I see no reason on why you changed my designation to Foliage Manager. I am really sorry. I am not going to your farm. I shall eat and watch television. The programmes are interesting. If I feel bored, I will just have a look at the seas. In the meantime, Mr. Narayanan, "arrange for my return tickets to India".

That was the first argument. I got a fax message saying that I would be given the right job in a fortnight's time and hence I should manage with the situation right now.

I thought that was fair and began driving to his farm. Just imagine, I get a letter stating that I am inefficient and hence my salary would be deducted by 2000 J$. (Well, he did not know who I was). I now fully understood his intentions. That bastard has not been blessed with any children. Why, because he has been doing this to many people. Calling people to work and harassing them ; mostly the Indians.

The second argument was more serious. This time, he had sent one of his Directors to sort out the problem for me. The discussion was so fierce that in no way would I agree on their decisions nor come to a compromise. I made it clear to the white men, that they would not be able to play their dirty tricks on me. I very well told them that I was a professional with more than a decade of experience. I spoke to the management and said to one of its Directors "If you are really holding some power and if you call yourself a director. . . . . . . I pity you. You are also one among us. Afterall you are paid, I mean you get your salary from that bastard. "Go tell him that he cannot pluck a single hair from my underball". We will have to meet in the court or I would be forced to take asylum at the Indian High Commissioner's office. I would want to see and put an end to this.

Well, I got my 2000 J$ refunded. The scoundrel wanted to have a private discussion with me. He flew all the way from the States. I really don't know why he was so polite. He asked on what works I was interested. Although he was polite, I knew he was a tricky person and hence maintained my temperament. "What the hell are you asking?" "You know my work permit was applied for the post of an Engineer, you are now talking as though you are totally new to it". . . . . Well, I don't want *to discuss anything more with you. "Where are my return tickets? I wanted to leave your wretched company".*

Somehow, I cooled down and we had come to a conclusion. I agreed on handling a few technical works in the farm. This time it was my time to be tricky. I kept a cool head. I knew he was not going to provide me with the tickets nor put me in the right job. I knew what do do. Make friends with him and then betray him for all the things he had done to me. I was really smart enough in not signing any of his documents. I was always careful and thought twice before signing any paper.

In the meantime, I was seriously trying for a job in other parts of the country. I am either considered too qualified or not qualified for the jobs I apply. Well, I came across this somewhere. . . . . EARN. . . . . INVEST. . . . . & GROW. I got a satisfactory job relevent to my field and experience.

I wrote to Narayanan saying we will have to meet in the court. Every document of his would go against him. Hence, it would be the best to come to a consensus. He again flew down to the country from the United States. This time the arguments were serious.

He had spent money for my travel. I wanted to leave his company. He says he had incurred a loss. But what about my loss. I was holding a responsible post in India. I was doing my own business. You were the one who bought me all the way from India and cheated me. Well, the argument was that I pay him the money he spent so that he would legally apply for a "NOC" (No objection certificate). Well, I don't have the money nor intend to pay you was my reply. I made it very clear to him that as on that day, I intend not to work for him any more and he could handle it anywhere he wished. (I am hundred percent sure, he would not want to make any more issues out of this because I have all valid documents that would go against him).

Well, that was it. He let me go freely. I am quite happy. Its almost six months since I have been on my own. I mean, since I had left the old wretched guy. Things had been a bit difficult for some time. But with the blessings of you all and my confidence and God's guidance I have been progressing well. I have saved about half of hundred thousand dollars. Now this money that I have saved is only for emergency. I had told you about my future plans. Well, now that I have saved the money and deposited in a fixed account, I am now happy that I can start sending you some money. The money that I earn from now would not go to the bank but I intend to save it and send them to you. Well to be frank with you, I had undergone great pains in the saving of the money. Now, I am really happy that I have become self-secured. I mean, even if I don't work, I could always be happy with the interest @ 20 % I get every month on the money that I have deposited.

To be very frank with you, it was only yesterday (29. 3. 1996) that I opened the account. Till such time I had to be very careful in putting the money in the suitcase. Well, I should not build any positive hopes for you people. But I really know what has to be done. So you will have to wait. I will have to start saving as on April 1, 1996 to do something good for you all. You should note that I have decided not to touch the money that I have deposited in the bank nor intend to send you any out of the same. As I feel secure and happy with the money in the bank.

Any how hopefully I shall start sending my contribution shortly.

Convey my regards to all the near and dear ones.

HOME SWEET HOME

MISSING THE BIG PLATE OF BRINJAL SAMBHAR

POTATO CURRY, RASAM AND CURD.

Continuation of the letter the next day on 2.4.1996

I would have posted this letter earlier. But, its good I did not. Well, I got your telegram. I really don't see any reason on why you trouble me with your telegrams. Any how, I already told you that the area where I stay has no telephone facility. There has been some major cabling problem and its almost an year since the residents of the area have been managing without the telephone. Now, a few miles away from this place, people have telephones but no "international call" facility. Tell me, how you expect me to get in touch with you. I had to travel all the way to a different parish and spent about 450 $ to make a call to you. I had to go to the Jamaican telephone company to avail the facility. There was a restriction of only 3 minutes. The whole day has been full of tension for me! If you people think I am just spending my money on drinking, sex, etc., let me tell you frankly I hardly have time for it nor could I afford for such things. In reading my letter, you would really appreciate my hardships in the savings which I have kept for emergencies.

You may all be anxious and surely you may want to get some benefits because I am abroad. Please understand things have been very difficult for me. I have just started picking up. You people don't understand my problem. Let me get it straight to you people :

(1) When did I leave India ? It was during June 22, 1995.

(2) What was the salary I was getting in Narayanan's company ? 6500 J$ - Taxes = 5500 J$

(3) How much do you think I could have saved ? NOTHING.

(4) When did I leave Narayanan ? During November 1995.

(5) Between November 1995 till date, well I could save some money.

(6) *Assuming I was in Narayanan's company, you could have anticipated Rs. 75,000/-. That too only at the end of June 1996.*

(7) *Now let me ask you something, how the hell on earth are you expecting something from me so early.*

Now, let me make things clear to you. If you are in real need of money,

(1) *Make use of the credit cards to the maximum or*

(2) *Ask Raghu/Hema/Gnanasekar to arrange for some loan on a reasonable interest. Or*

(3) *Talk to my old boss in Gremach and tell him your requirements and he will arrange it for you. (I would not prefer this.)*

I promise you that I shall settle all your dues till the last penny, in a very short time. (with the present situation, I am sure I can transfer 50,000 J$ during the first week of August 1996. I can surely promise you on this. In the meantime, if any changes occur, I will keep you informed.

Continuation of the same letter on 5.4.1996

Well, I really don't know why this letter is being delayed. I sent this letter to the post office but got it back because I was told the postal rates are up from 1. 80 J$ to about 50 J$. I am afraid if I could keep up my commitment as mentioned to you in my earlier letter that I would be writing to you every week effective April 1. Now, I am sure I would get my telephone by the end of April or early May 1996. Till such time you should have patience. Please don't send telegrams and bother me. Once I have the telephone facility, I would be contacting you once in a week (i.e.) On every Saturday/Sunday.

Regarding the finance, as I had told you earlier, check for a loan, if you are in real need. I am expecting about 50-75,000 J$ during August 1996. If you can wait till such time, both of us could be happy.

I once again confirm to you all, that if you are in real need of money, Raghu should be able to get some quick loan. I promise that I shall settle his loan with interest during August 1996.

Please bear with me and wait till I call you with my personal telephone shortly.

Till such time, bye.

It took considerable time to read Babu's letter. And it took still longer time to digest the facts mentioned in it. My blood started to boil and my anger over Babu's aggressive behaviour grew sky-high. As usual, he had lost his temper! And this time, it was in a foregin land, where there were even no friends or relatives to defend him. How daring he must have been to start a row and challenge Narayanan, his boss, who was wholly responsible for bringing him to Jamaica. Did he not know that the boss was always right ? Well, if Narayanan was really in the wrong, Babu could have tackled him in a more matured manner! He should have been prudent enough and known how to come out of the precarious situation that he had got entangled into, by playing it safe. If he was not satisfied with his job, he could have silently kept this to himself and without grumbling should have made enough money and left the country, instead of blowing it out of proportion, by defying his boss. By giving vent to his anger and getting into the bad books of Narayanan, he was heading for trouble.

In an over confident manner, he proudly states that he could tide over any situation in life! In fact, he has totally ruined his life. And it was not just his life that was at stake but his family down here in India, who were wholly dependent on him, were also getting to naught.

Surely, the family was drifting away from his mind. Otherwise, he would not have acted in a very nonchalant manner, unmindful of whatever was happening back at home. Besides, he was also irked by our letters and telegrams and had requested us not to bother him with our telegrams.

Another thing that provoked me was his breach of promise. Everytime, he keeps promising that he would send us money but is unable to keep his word for some reason or the other. I started to fear if he had forgotten the very purpose for which he left India. It is almost a year now after leaving India and he had not helped us by giving a single pie.

I just could not appreciate Babu's assertiveness nor his audacious ways in dealing with his problems in a foreign land. I could also not comprehend as to why father was asking me not to write in detail to Babu about Raghu's crazy behaviour of constantly borrowing money from one source or the other and thus ruining the family's peace. By keeping Babu in the dark about this, I did not know whether we were doing the right thing or the wrong. But as usual, I decided to be his obedient daughter and blindly obliged him. May be father feared that if we apprise him of the impoverished conditions of the family, he would get angry and not send any money at all.

Suddenly, I became downhearted and a gloomy future lurking ahead of us petrified me. I decided to air my views to Babu, denouncing his disagreeable attitude.

23

A Dismal Picture

I had been fully absorbed in drafting my reply to Babu; taking every care to make it a complaisant one. My intention was not to hurt him in any way but to make him realize that if he did not give up his temper he would not be able to shine in life. In fact, I wished to point out to him that his anger would not let him climb up the social ladder. He had to change himself and learn to adjust to the circumstances he was in. Even before sending my letter to him, we received another letter from Babu. In this letter, he had expressed his dissatisfaction and the problems he was currently facing in Jamaica and repented for having left his motherland in the first place :

Hope this letter of mine finds you in good health and prosperity. Well, things for me have rather been tough and am afraid are still going to be the same way. The cost of living is increasing day by day. The business that I am doing as you know is not doing that well. It just keeps me going. I am yet to secure myself. I really think it was a wrong decision to come all the way from India to Jamaica without enquiring the general details about the country. The main problem is the devaluation of the Jamaican dollar. Any how that's not our problem.

To be frank with you, I am not satisfied with this country. I mean the saving potential. For example, if you invest about 1000 J$ in a finance institution and you expect to get about 1200 J$ by the month end, the inflation goes up to 300 J$. I really don't know if you would understand the problem. Jobs in this country are only on temporary basis. The policy is "hire and fire". If you really need a job, you would hardly get about 5000 J$ - 8000 J$ in the countryside and in the town it varies between 50000 J$ to 80,000 J$. But the town is a terrorist area. You can almost hear daily about robberies, gun shots, etc. Jamaica is one of the countries in the world where maximum number of murders take place. Well you know this is a free country and the repurcussions of this could be well imagined. Although I go to the town once a month or so, I really don't have any problem. As long as you don't look big in the city, you are safe.

I really don't know when things are going to stabilize. The country is ofcourse good. It is closer to the United States. Countries like Cuba, Trinidad and Tobago, Barbados, Dominican Republic, Bahamas are just an hours journey from here. Well all these are only tourist spots.

Well, that was the reason why I had decided to not work for any company. We had started a company as you know by the name of "Kens Associates Ltd". The legal papers of Registration are yet to come but the operations of the company are going on. Well, I work for one day on AC systems and make as good as 10,000 J$ a day. But the jobs are not consistent. I am really happy that I don't have to work for any company, from 9.00 a.m. to 5.00 p.m. or so. Well, the advantage of my being on business is I don't have any timings, the money that I would get for the whole month working for any company, I get it in a day.

You may ask what the hell is then wrong with this guy. Yes, the question seems to be logical and good in the sense that *it would look like I earn but not support you all. Listen, If I have to send money to you, I can do it only in the form of US dollars and not Jamaican dollars. Now, if I have to buy 1 US dollar, I have to spend 40 J$. I. e. 40 J$ = 1 US $*

Now in India, 1 US $ = 32. 50 Indian Rupees.

Now work out the loss I would incur, if I plan to send about 100 US $, I have to spend 4000 J$. But you would get only Rs. 3250/-

I have not taken the transaction/service charges into account. You very well know, the postal rates have got up from 1. 50 J$ to 48 J$. I should not bore you up with figures. I should be frank in admitting this to you all. If I were to be in Jamaica

and no one depending on me, I should have been happy and the struggle would be nothing. Now the problem is you are depending on me for finance and I am really in pain thinking of how I would do this. The loss I would incurr is going to be large. Well, as I had written to you earlier, I plan to keep my commitment at any cost and till such time you may have to manage. Shortly, I was informed that your letter dated 13. 1. 1996 has reached the old address. I will have to get in touch with the old office to receive it.

Now, regarding the telephone facility, I don't know what my luck is. My plans are failing badly. Whenever I am sure of something good to happen, it always turns the other way round. I don't know why. Is it a curse by someone on me ? I ask myself. For sure, I know it should have been the wretched guy in the States. But God knows who is right. In fact I would be highlighting the problem to the Labour Department.

I am really happy from the fact that I have gained one year of experience abroad. Now, even if I come back to India, stay at home for a few months, and then try for a job in the Gulf, it would be very easy for me to get a job.

I had plans to stay in Jamaica for atleast five years. I think the situation in Jamaica is getting worse. I don't see any kind of future prospects in this country. Let me see if I could manage for another one year. If I should, I think I could think of the future stay.

As you all know, I don't give up that easily and challenges are more interesting. Obviously without your prayers I think things would be different.

I shall write to you more in my next letter, till such time, take care.

If at all his letter gave me any happiness, it was the time he had devoted for us, in penning this letter. His letter did very little to erase out the melancholic mood that I was encompassed with. For the facts mentioned in it were so dismal and unpalatable to read. It deprived me of any hope I had that he would send some money in the near future.

24

The News That Spread Like a Wild Fire

One evening, not having anything better to do, I was sitting on the steps, watching my daughter play. Suddenly, the phone shrilled and when the ringing tone was a lengthy one, I doubled over to pick it up, with my heart in my mouth, for I was sure that it was from none other than Babu. And when I heard Babu's voice ; after a pretty long time, adrenalin surged my viens. I just could not believe that it was my brother on the other end. His voice had totally changed. He spoke like a foreigner and I was finding it quiet difficult to understand his accent.

At last, he gave me the much awaited news. He told me that he had transferred a sum of Rs. 50,000/- into father's account. He also gave us his contact phone number and asked me to inform him once father received the money.

As I placed the receiver on the cradle, my face lit up with a smile. I divulged the news to my mother and she was excited too. And when father returned from his walk, I happily told him about Babu's phone call. Though father was delighted to hear the news, he was quick to make a sarcastic comment, "after nearly two years, he is sending us just Rs. 50,000/-! And look at the commitments we have!" Father was never satisfied, when it came to money! He always wanted far more!

The news that Babu was going to send money spread like wild fire. All of us were wondering as to what exactly father intended to do with the money. Each of us had a dream and we were building castles in the air. Usha believed that father would buy jewels for her marriage. I expected that father would atleast give a part of it towards the loan he had borrowed from us on behalf of Raghu. So far, I had almost shelled out Rs. 40,000/- which had become the cause of frequent quarrels between my husband and me. I hoped that if I repayed atleast a part of the loan, our disputes would reduce. My brother Raghu however did not have any such plans. He was confident that father would spend the entire money in repaying his loans.

The car business which Raghu started resulted in a tremendous loss to the family. He was unable to make his monthly payments of his car loan nor could he afford to spend money on its repairs. Due to this, the car did not give him any profit and the loan amount kept increasing. Hence, Raghu was forced to sell the car. There were no takers for this second hand car and finally, he sold it for Rs. 1 lakh at a loss of Rs. 70,000/-. At a young age of Twenty Four years, he had already an outstanding loan of more than Rs. 2 lakhs.

Raghu was of a very peculiar character. After taking loans from each and every person known to him, he never bothered to repay the same or rather he thought that it was not his responsibility. He would shun them completely and dodge their payments. But if he was able to get on well with this idiosyncrasy, it was because of his cool disposition. Unlike Babu, he never lost his temper! Any kind of threatening or harsh words spoken by the lenders would not deter him. He would be unruffled and talk to people in a composed manner and tide over the crisis in an amicable way.

On the day father received the money, Raghu went and sat down in front of him and said, "after Babu left for Jamaica, you had shifted the entire family burden on to my shoulders. For almost two years now, Babu had sent nothing and since I was also out of job, I tried my luck at the car business. Unfortunately, the business did not run well and now as per your advice, I have sold the car. I had no other go but to keep borrowing money from one source or the other with an intention of doing good to the family and that Babu would solve our money problem one day or the other. I am now being hounded from all sides for return of their money and I request you to help me out. " He left father with no option and as usual, father gave in to his sweet-talk.

My sister Usha was fuming. Though it was already four years after my marriage, father was not able to find a suitable alliance for her. She was turning into an irksome person and gave vent to her anger by screaming at everybody for no reason at all.

Though I felt bad about father's uncaring attitude in not repaying my loan, I did not express my disappointment at this. For, I was too much occupied with the construction of my house, which was nearing completion. On 26th November 1996, I performed the house warming ceremony in a very gala manner. On that day, if at all I had some thing to regret about, it was the absence of my brother Babu. But then, I convinced myself that, the moment he returned to India, I could invite him and show off my grand house to him.

25

Man Proposes and God Disposes

Babu had given me his telephone number and asked me to inform him once we received the money. But I never did. There were two reasons for this. One, the telepone charges were too high and if I spoke to him for even two minutes, I would have to shell out Rs. 150/-. The other reason was that ; if Babu asked me how the money was spent by father, I did not have an apt answer. I did not wish to lie to him that it was usefully spent nor tell him the truth that the entire money was taken off by Raghu to repay his loans.

I left the task of informing Babu, about the receipt of money, to father. And father, wrote a long letter to him. He told him about the pending electricity bills, the disconnected telephone line, and about the extreme poverty conditions that still continued to exist in the family eversince he left. But father was too clever ; for no where in the letter did he make a mention, as to how the money sent by him was actually spent.

We were now eagerly waiting to hear from Babu. But Babu never called up nor did we receive any letter from him. My efforts in trying to contact him also met with failure. I was struck with panic as to what had happened to him. I longed to see him! I wanted him to come back to India. I had thought that Babu's going abroad would make my family rich! Now, I lost all hope! The family was going from bad to worse every day. I believed that if Babu returned to India, he would take over the burden and I shall be free from any responsibility.

After nearly a period of six months, during the month of October, I felt much relieved when the postman stopped by and delivered an air-mail envelope. My fears were allayed and my restiveness eased a little. As I read Babu's letter dated 13. 9. 1996, I was fretting and fuming at his careless behaviour in not trying to contact us, so far.

Hope this letter of mine finds you in good health and high spirits. Its really a long time since I had written to you. I am sorry. I was involved in a major project. The project has neared completion. I am back in my parish. Well, I really did find the time now to write to you all. Well, life has been rough but the struggle has been quite interesting. I always thank the Lord that my life has been a "Bed of thorns" and not a "Bed of roses". I had learnt so much in life. I have learnt the value of money.

Now, I ask myself, should I still struggle in Jamaica or come back to India and stay with you all for a couple of months and then leave to some other country. Incidentally, I should tell you that I have sent my curriculam vitae to "Dubai". In case I get some positive response, I would love to come back to India, stay with you all for atleast a couple of months and then leave to the Middle East. But you know nothing is in our hands, "Man Proposes and God disposes".

Now, let me not bore you up with my struggles in life. I am a person who does not give up. I have my own ambitions and goals in life. I am sure I would be able to reach my goal with the blessings of God and you all. But the funniest thing is when I climb my ladder trying to cross one step, the devil pulls me back by two steps. I hope you understand. Making money (I would prefer saying making rather than earning) is very difficult in Jamaica. But spending is very easy. The cost of living is increasing day by day. Nothing is easy here.

I am sure, after my stay here, I would be a better man and can work in any country with ease. I am learning so much that life would not be difficult for me in future. I have become a more calmer person, more matured, better in communication, learned to work under pressure, lastly but not the least to remain calm under heavy pressure or stress. What more experience would you want. Well, I tell myself "Sam - with this experience, you are going to be a big man one day!".

I always thank the Lord for whatever I am today. He has been guiding me in the right direction. I know if at all there is any obstacle, it is for my good and better prospects. One thing I would like to tell you all is not to bother or worry about me. I know how to deal with any kind of person, any kind of situation.

Well, how are things at home ? How is Vinodini doing at school ? How is mother's health ? How is the progress in Hemalatha's construction ? What has happened to Usha's marriage ? How are Ramesh, Raghu and Gnanasekar ?

I think I might come home during the end of this year. Might be Usha's marraige has been pending just because of my absence. I would love to be a member of the team in organizing things for her wedding. But when I am back home, I would not prefer coming back to Jamaica. I don't see any better prospects in this country. Most probably I would like to travel to the Middle East. Lets see what happens.

I thought I could send some money this month and ask you to start the construction of our house i. e. the first floor and the extension of the Ground Floor. The devil has spoilt all my plans. But any how, I know I would make it and am sure the Lord would bless me in all my endeavours.

I would write to you more in my next letter. Take care, till we get in touch!

***P. S** : I do hope the money that I sent has been spent usefully. As I had told you earlier the money was sent exclusively for Usha only. Hope all things required for her wedding have already been purchased.*

I hope you have found some one suitable for her. Well, let me ask you something. You know how old I am. Do you think I can wait any longer. I think you should know better. I am looking for a good , nice looking girl. Will I find her in Jamaica or in India ? I think I should start finding one in Jamaica and not depend on any one of you.

Somehow, I felt that as long as Babu was here, there was no dearth of food in the family and more important than that, there were no loans to be paid. Father never liked to borrow and had maintained the family so well. But now, every one was after Raghu ; who in turn was coolly directing them to my parents. My parents were having a tough time in convincing them about the delay in payment of their dues and it was indeed a very embarrassing moment for them. The fact that Babu was planning to come back to India filled me with immense joy. Atleast then, Raghu's cranky behaviour of borrowing money and further ruining the family would come to an abrupt end!

26

This is Not a Joke

After reading Babu's letter ; which arrived after a pretty long time, I was left with a doubt! Did he read all the letters that father had been sending to him. During these six months, irrespective of the fact that Babu was not replying to his letters, father had been constantly writing to him enlightening him about the penury conditions prevailing in the family. My doubts were very soon cleared! For this letter (29. 10. 1996) which we received in quick succession, was nothing but an eruption of his strong feeling of displeasure and indignation at all of us.

"How the hell on earth. . . . . . " I am sorry for having started my letter with such harsh words. But any how I should go ahead. "How the hell on earth, did you people not have the courtesy to say thanks to the money that I sent ? How much did you receive ? What did you do with it ? Not a single word has been mentioned in your so called five page letters. You people don't seem to write what is really expected. Do you know how hard it was for me to make that little money. I had sent 1400 US $. Any how, how was it spent ?

Why is it you people always cry for money. Always complain about electricity bill and telephone bill. It is a real shame on your part. Please don't tell me these stories in future. I am fed up of it. Do you want to listen to my story. Who do I ask for electricity money or telephone money ? Who do I ask for money in case of emergency ? Who do I ask money to fill up my gas tank ? Well, let me not irritate you people. I would have been happy if you had atleast mentioned that you received ____ and you have spent it on ____. Its real pity that there was hardly any mention about it! Why ? The first thing on receiving this letter, please make it clear, on what has been spent on behalf of Usha's marriage.

Also, I keep getting the same message about Usha's marriage. I am fed up of it. Don't write anything more about your trial or what so ever it is, till you finalise. Hope you finalise her marriage before Vinu comes of age. It is again a shame on your part. Before going to bed, ask yourself the following questions :

If Usha finds someone suitable and runs away from the house would you be happy ? Do you want our relatives and your friends to talk about her, saying she has some incurable disease ? Probably I should blame Hemalatha for all this. Might be she is very selfish and wicked in thoughts. She would understand what I mean.

If I had a chance to see on how you proceed with each of the alliance that seems to fail, I would have exactly known who's fault it was. But anyhow, since you are the organiser, you are to be blamed.

Stop bothering about me. I don't have a permanent address ; I don't have a telephone. "I have money" ! Thank the lord for it! I have a house, rather a cabin to stay. I am hail and healthy. I would be happy to have your advice after you finalise

Usha's marriage. Till such time, I don't need any of your advice. Please don't bother about my nature of job, income etc.

I keep telling you that I am not a kid, the Lord has always been guiding me in the direction that ; in spite of the burdens, life has not been miserable. The burdens are not that heavy to shoulder. I am an engineer, would be an engineer and would stay as an engineer. Why do you people fret about my job. Don't you people know that I am a person with self-prestige, over confidence and good technical skills. How do you think I could change my field ? Why do you keep asking me this again and again.

Any how I am really sick of this country. I need to come back home. I need to eat, Sambhar rice thrice, Rasam rice twice and curd rice. I am fed up of the rotten food I eat in Jamaica. I would say junk food. My tongue is almost dead, lost taste and well, people say I have put on some weight, but I am not sure as yet.

Money is a problem for everyone on earth. You have money problem, I have money problem, The world has money problem. It is better to shut our mouth rather than to expose it. The day you expose it, you lose your respect. Although I am not that rich (rather not that poor), people come to me and ask for loans. I just cannot stop laughing. The entire community where I live think that I am a rich and wealthy man. I hardly have a dollar in my pocket, but people call me the "Money man". Sometimes, I ask them, why they feel I have more money. They say my face tells it. I don't know what the hell is written on my face.

Anyhow, I feel pity for you all. I would be sending about Rs. 20,000 by the last week of November 1996 or earlier, towards the pending telephone bills, electricity bills and other miscellaneous expenditure. Well, I shall add another Rs. 5000 especially for my mother for her Deewali expenses. Don't fret. Thank the Lord for everything you have.

Please make your expenses worthwhile. "EARNING IS DIFFICULT, SPENDING IS EASY". This trip that I had made to Jamaica is only an experience. When I come back to India, I would not have any money or savings. The only savings I would have is the adequate experience. But with this experience, when I come back home / India, get married and leave to some other country, I am sure, all my savings would go for different endeavours in terms of business / housing / social purposes. Well, I don't have any regrets. If I had been in India, it would have still been a hand to mouth situation. As a result, it really does not make a difference. The only difference is that I am missing you all. But this time when I come to India and decide to go to a different country, I would be choosy. You know I would have a title saying that I am an "Overseas Returnee , more weightage, more money and you know it would be more easy for me to get into any country. Any how "Man proposes and God disposes". Let us see what would happen and hope for best things to happen, leaving our trust to the almighty lord.

Please make sure that mother gets Rs. 5000 / - in cash, when you receive the money during November. I hope you could buy "Vinu" some thing special. Things are costly here. Let me add another Rs. 5000 / - for her. i. e. I would be sending about Rs. 30,000 / -. Buy her what she needs. Best of luck.

My blood pressure shot up as soon as I finished reading the letter. Babu had called father shameless for not settling Usha's marriage so far. He had also called me selfish and wicked. Besides, he had added a clause to that : *She would understand what I mean.* I was really perplexed. One thing, I was not sure as to what he meant by that statement and the other was I wondered where exactly I had gone wrong. What made him call me selfish? For eversince he left India, I had been taking care of the family. I had been doing everything in my capacity to look into the comforts of my family and turn them into a rich family! In fact, that is why, he was himself in Jamaica in the first place. But however, my plans were not turning out so well. God was challenging me for the attachment I had to the family and for the interference in others' lives. He was punishing me and teaching me lessons to mind my own business and not interfere. And I was finding it hopeless to fight against Him. I was a silent victim to everything that was happening in my family! I could not stop its destruction in any manner! I had given more than Rs. 50,000/- to my father for repayment of loans for which I was being called selfish. Babu's words hurt my feelings beyond relief. While I kept pondering over his harsh words, a few thoughts passed my mind. It occurred to me that my detached and uncaring attitude in finding Usha a suitable alliance might have probably provoked him. Well, Babu was coming to India by the middle of May 1997. Before that, I had to finalise Usha's marriage, come what may. I told Usha that since the construction of my house was now over, I would pray to God and find a good match for her very soon. But Usha considered this as a joke. I then vouched to her that this was no joke and I was quite serious about this. However, I told her that it would take three months to settle her marriage. And she laughed.

Once again, I turned to God. I offered my fervent prayers to Him requesting for settlement of my sister's marriage!

27

A Mind Boggling Issue

Wonder of wonder! My sister's marriage was finalised within the allotted time slot that I had promised her. I thanked my sister and mother for taking care of my daughter lovingly for the last five years. Now that I had a house of my own, I brought down my daughter and put her in a school near my house. The next project in my agenda was to have my second child. This time I longed to have a son. All of us here were looking forward to Babu's arrival to India during May 1997.

During the fag end of 1996, we received a letter from him in which he had once again elaborated the problems faced by him in Jamaica. His letter dated 30. 12. 1996 read as follows:

Hope this letter of mine finds you all in good health and high spirits. Got all your messages / telegrams / fax. All these messages, however, make me feel that you have all lost your normal senses. Especially Raghu who is dealing with credit cards and loans. If you are going to take a loan without even keeping me informed, it would not make any sense in seeking help from me. Its total foolishness. One of the messages sent was stating that a loan of Rs. 2,00,000/- is due. Why the hell was this money borrowed. Who do you want to blame for this foolishness ?

Anyhow, you were lucky that I had some money to send. I had sent US $ 750 on the 13. 12. 1996. Hope you had received the money and spent it usefully. You may have to regret that it would be impossible for me to send any more money till the mid of 1997. All my savings have diminished. I am really wondering if you people have any conscience in spending. You may have to think once/twice before doing any shopping.

About myself, I am yet to take a decision on when to return back to India. "Competition exists all over the Middle East & India." Is it going to be wise in staying here or return as per my plan is the question, I am unable to answer. If I get the right job with the right company my minimum salary would be J$ 40,000 with all perks. The present situation with me is that I am self employed. To get the right job, I may have to change my work permit or change my "STATUS". To change the status is easy but I am still under very serious consideration. To change the permit would be difficult as I am still having the possession of the same work permit applied by the guy (Narayanan). I will soon take a decision and let you know. Please note my bank balance is "NIL" as on date as I have sent all the money that I had to you. You will surely agree with me that the first instance when I had sent US$ 1400, the service charges/transaction charges were borne by me. Even during this transaction (US $ 750), all expenses were borne by me. Well, you should know how much I should have paid as service charges (its my one month's expenses for food). The only plus point with me is that I don't complain nor tell you my difficulties. Being self-employed, I am totally exhausted, almost tired everyday. I have to do the marketing, sales, service, maintenance, installation. To make it easy for you all to understand, let me tell you that I am a consultant, engineer, manager, director, technician, mechanic *and helper. The company is mine and I cannot bother myself in appointing anyone to assist me as I cannot afford it. Might be if I take a decision in changing my "STATUS" (Marital) things could change. I could get a job very easily as I would be naturalised / domiciled to Jamaica. I can invite any one of you to come to this country. But one thing, I have serious thoughts about changing my status. I will soon make a decision. Before that I will take all pains to renew my work permit. Let's see how it goes.*

In the meantime, I should tell you a very interesting story. I was selected by a company in North America as a "Resident Services Engineer". They had spent about Rs. 40,000/- in processing all my papers and air tickets. I was really so happy and thought God had really helped me out of the crisis situation that I was facing. I had to fly on the 5. 11. 1996. I had packed up all my belongings, said good bye to all my friends and neighbours and left to the airport with my tickets and passport. At the American Airlines there was a sweet lady who on seeing all my papers / passport so politely told me that I cannot fly as I don't have the "American Visa". I was so disappointed. I had to call the people in North America and informed them of the proceedings. They were so professional that again they helped with a few changes in the documents. Now, I had to go to the "American Embassy" to apply for the VISA. The white fellow in the Embassy turned down my "VISA" application. Since I could not get my "VISA", I could not make my trip. I had to send back the Air tickets, cancel all arrangements. Well, its a very sorry story. But I would not give up. So is life. As long as there is breath in us, problems are bound to exist. The more problems one has, the more alive he his. If one has no problems, it means he is not having any life in him. Hope, I write to you atleast once a fortnight. Bye for now!

Babu had given us the shocking news that he did not have sufficient funds to purchase his air-tickets to return to

India during May 1997. Further, the fact that he was planning to change his status (by getting married) to prolong his stay, was mind-boggling to me. He also started to believe in the fact that, the more problems one had, the more alive he is. And if one has no problems, it means he is not having life in him. While his thinking was indeed mature, I despised the fact that he was probably taking things in a very cool manner. Ruination of his family back home in India, did not mean anything to him. Surely, his mind was getting distracted!

28

God Helps Those Who Help Themselves

Whatever money Babu sent to father, it really never got into his hands. It was taken up by Raghu to pay up his never-ending dues. Hence, father kept writing one letter after another, requesting Babu to send more money for his day to day expenses. However, in all his letters, father took great care to not let out the queer nature of Raghu. Nor did he divulge the facts as to why such a huge sum was borrowed. This infuriated Babu so much and he kept calling us names and expressing his anger.

On the other hand, I considered father's intention to keep the eccentricity of Raghu a secret, as merely nonsensical. Babu had hurt my feelings by calling me selfish. There was no point in hiding the facts from him anymore. I decided to disclose everything that was happening back at home, to Babu. I wished to disobey father and let the cat out of the bag. Without father's knowledge, I wrote a long letter to Babu revealing everything to him. I wrote about Raghu's purchase of a second hand car which has resulted in the downfall of the family.

But very soon, I had to repent for my hasty decision. My letter had aroused his anger to an insurmountable degree and in the following letter dated 24. 1. 1997, he had spelt out his fury by individually addressing each one of us.

Dear Mr. Gnanasekar, (My husband)

Hope this note of mine finds you in good harmony. However, I would like to make my note very brief. I see no reason on why the expenditure in our house has reached to massive dues. Raghu is immature and does not know what exactly he his doing. Why don't you suggest and make good recommendations on what to buy and what not to buy. I don't see the reason on why a car was purchased on a loan. If he already owed the bank lots of money, why the hell on earth should he buy a car. The worst is why should he sell it at a huge loss. Don't you think this is total foolishness ? To be very frank ; I am not in a position to help for these foolish expenditures ; neither do I want you to encourage this kind of foolishness.

Have you any time realized that with the outstanding dues, a big wedding could be conducted. I mean Usha's marriage. No body thinks about this. Please advise Raghu to cancel all his credit cards. You have really encouraged him by lending him a big sum of money. Who do you think is going to return the money to you ? Positively not me. Just imagine, if his monthly salary is about Rs. 4000/-, how can he think of bigger things. What the hell has been purchased through the credit cards ?

This is totally ridiculous. I am sorry to hear this. I really thought you would have been playing a leading role in taking decisions. But does not look so. Well, I believe you have the funds to encourage Raghu in all foolish purchases. Encourage him and let's see where it ends!

Dear Hemalatha,

You can neither take a decision on your own nor would suggest anything good to people. How could you (I know it should have been you) suggest the foolish idea of buying a car. Why the hell did he sell it for a loss ? You think I am going to take up the loss. You people should be joking! Even if I had the money, I would never do such a foolish thing. What the hell is Raghu purchasing through credit cards. Don't you ever ask yourself if the family is justified in spending money on his foolishness. Well, since you are a part of this foolishness, you may have to pay for the consequences. Pay him, encourage him and ruin the family.

Dear Vinu, (my daughter)

I am really sorry for you. This uncle of yours is an unlucky guy. I have not sent a chocolate since I left you. To be frank, I don't feel sorry for you, I feel sorry for myself. But I am sure, you would be taken care of in a nice manner. Hope you are doing well at school. I have something special for you which I would be sending sooner or later. I wish you all good luck.

Dear Usha, (my sister)

I am not in a position to write anything to you ; except my regrets. In every letter of mine, I always try to make sure that I am in haste to get married. You should well know the reason. I thought atleast then your marriage would be fixed ; atleast then father would try to rush things ; atleast then, you will try to find a match for yourself early. You are now 30 years old. All the hardwork and help you have been doing for the family! While I used to get up early in the morning and rush to Thiruninrarur, you used to wake me up with a cup of coffee and I used to have the best food. I can't see a person like this wasting her youth. But one thing , please keep in mind! If at all I keep mentioning about my marriage, it is only to create a stress on yours. I am in no hurry. I would never want to be married, if just sex was my thought. Well, if you are happy with your decisions and if you are happy with all that's happening, I don't care a foot for your welfare. I have no business in forcing your issue. This is the last time, I am mentioning about your marriage. Never will I again. Because, it so has an effect, that others think I am mad for getting married.

Dear Ramesh, (my youngest brother)

You are lucky. I cannot blame you for anything. Because you are always sure on what you do. You and mother are a pair and I know nothing could go wrong. Well, I hope you are getting on well with your job and do hope there would be some hike in your salary very soon. I want you to write to me clearly on what's happening in the house. Why is there so much of confusion ? Take care of my bike. Well, you know its yours. Sometimes, I think it would have been better to be like you without any responsibilities. It would have been better, if I had not travelled abroad. Even, if I come back, I am not going to travel anymore. I am just going to eat and sleep.

Dear Mother,

Amongst all the confusions and foolishness going on there; how is your health, B. P, Sugar......... Take care of your self and don't bother or involve with stupid arguments. Why don't you advise Raghu on expenses. I am sure you cannot be the cause for such huge dues. To be very frank with you all my savings had been transferred to India, during the couple of months and I am left with no money in my bank. Now, If I have to travel to India, I need 99,384 dollars. I don't have even a third of this. How is it you people depend on me so much ? You already know that I am self employed and earning my airfare / tickets to India by May 1997 is going to be very difficult. But I would make sure that after I come back, I shall not travel to any other country for the next five years. I am fed up of hard work and money. I need rest. All that I would do is to have good food, and sleep. I am not joking. I am very serious. Because you people think I am a money plant. One thing I could swear is that, if I was in India, I would have never allowed these dues to have built up.

Dear Father,

No use in going to the temple every evening and worshipping God. "God helps those who help themselves". If you cannot help yourselves, I see no point on why God should help you. I know you are a person who would always nod to people's suggestions and would never think on your behalf. Why is that you advised Raghu on an exhorbitant expenditure-with that money even if you had made the first floor or extended the front portion of the house, it would have been useful. Moreover it would be an asset. All of your letters seem to complain of money, money and money. Why ? What if I never existed? How the hell would you manage ? Well, I should have ignored the fax messages. But I tell you one thing, if I had the money, I would have atleast tried to help. But I hardly have any money. I am trying to make some money for my air tickets. I have just started. I just have a few thousand dollars and I cannot part that money on your foolishness. I am really fed up of all your decisions. You should suggest to Raghu to first of all cancel all the credit cards. Well, if not, you would see the result of the dues going to be built up.

Dear Raghu, (my second brother)

If provisions just cost Rs. 3000/- each month, all your figures mentioned in the fax totalling to nearly two lakhs seems to be having some misapprehensions.

What do the words "other home requirements" mean ? You already owe the banks big money. You are well educated. . . . . B. Com, DBM, MBA. Can't you manage a small responsibility. You should be stupid and ashamed of owing so much money to people. Well, do you think you were really smart in securing a bank loan 100 % to buy a second hand car ? Funny and ridiculous, about your immature thoughts.

Lastly Rs. 50,000/- from Gnansekar. In no way I am in a position to help. Think twice before spending even a dollar.

I am in need of 99,384 J$ to purchase my air tickets to India before May 1997. Can you help ? (Amount required before 31st May 1997 to avoid legal action or deportation)

I never imagined that my letter would have such an impact on Babu. It had literally maddened him. For, he had passed his adverse comments on each one of us. He did not like father's complete dependency on him to tide over the poverty life that we had brought upon ourselves due to negligence and laxity on our part.

On the other hand, the failure on his part to meet father's expectations made him speak disgustedly of him. When it came to money, father always wanted more! While I discussed about this letter with father, he was quick to comment, "it was all because of him that our family has come to naught. Believing that he would keep sending us money every month, we were in fact tempted in to borrowing huge loans with the hope that he would repay all the loans in the near future. After nearly two years of being away from home, he only sends a meagre sum of Rs. 50,000/-. And now he talks big and brags as if he has sent money in lakhs. Write to him that he is the sole cause of everything that is happening down here!"

I some how felt that I was to blame for all this. It was the repercussion of disobeying father and revealing the truth to him. Right now, Babu was planning to return to India and he was in shortage of money to buy his air-tickets. And I did not think it appropriate to air father's opinion which would hurt him and make him change his mind about his return to India. What if he decides to stay back in Jamaica itself? It had already been two years since I saw my brother and I was longing to see him. Money had all of a sudden become immaterial to me and I wished to see him at the earliest ; for I missed him a lot. Hence, I decided to write a letter to him and placate his intense anger he had over us.

29

Help in Conducting Marriage

I wrote a letter to Babu, about the ardent prayers I had offered in front of God with regard to Usha's marriage and the fruition of the same. Concomitantly, father wrote a separate letter to Babu apprising him in detail about settlement of Usha's marriage. He also elaborated upon the continuing financial crisis in the family, and requested him once again to help him in conducting Usha's marriage. But before our letters reached him, we received another letter from Babu , berating us.

Received your letter dated 20. 1. 1997 and noted the contents. I am really not able to understand your problems. Is there not a sensible person in the house who can deal with the problems intelligently. Well, what is the use of you people writing to me and narrating your foolish stories. Was I responsible for all the happenings there ? I am a human being like you people and not a money plant. I have sent around Rs. 1. 5 lakhs so far to you people and what did you do with that ? Out of this, only one necklace has been purchased for Usha. SHAME! SHAME!

Father can neither manage finance nor social affairs. Neither can he advice anything sensible. I thought my hard earned money would have been used for some good purpose. At least, if I had the money, I could have been happy with the interest amount and could have been well prepared to leave Jamaica during the end of the month.

Hemalatha seems to advise me on the happenings with Narayanan. Well, does not make any sense to me.

All expenses incurred due to the foolishness of Raghu have to be cleared by himself or those who helped him in his foolish act.

I neither have the money to part nor am I interested in those non-sensible, stupid, ridiculous, absurd, idiotic dealings.

Now, if father, mother, Usha or Hemalatha had a brain working, they would have done the following :

All of you know Raghu was dealing with stupid things. Remember! I sent the money to father so that he would have the total control. Until and unless he signs the cheque, no body can force him to release the money. But well, looks like all of you have lost your senses.

- *You could have asked Raghu to go to hell! Do what he wants and wishes but would not part with the money.*

- *Using the money that was transferred to father's account, every month Rs. 2000-3000 could have been drawn for purchase of provisions.*

- *If this was done, things should have been much better.*

- *I spent about 3000 J$ in making a long discussion over phone with you people before I sent the money to you.*

All waste. . . . . remember, the money earned was out of real hard work / risk and danger (electrical controls).

But, any how past is past and pray to Baba to help you all in the present and future.

I am planning to come down during the first / second week of May 1997.

All of you seem to think I am a God. Let me see what changes are going to happen when I come back.

A word to father :

On my arrival to India, I would be landing at Bombay and would like to travel by train and reach Madras. However, I plan to stay in Bombay for a couple of days before I reach Madras. I would like to explore my market in Bombay (agencies). I am still not sure about this. But shall confirm to you shortly.

The fact that Babu was planning to return to India during May 1997 filled me with great joy. I was looking forward to see him. Once he returns, all my burdens will be gone. I would then be bereft of problems concerning my family.

30

An Absurd Idea

The month of May had come and gone ; but Babu did not return home as promised. Father was breaking his head with regard to the mounting financial pressures and was wondering how he was going to perform Usha's marriage. One day he discussed the subject of Usha's marriage with Raghu, and as usual, he came up with one of his absurd ideas of pledging the house. Father was left with no other option and he agreed to do the same. However, he decided to talk to Babu about this. Babu was indeed happy to hear the good news about Usha's marriage. He told father to go ahead with the pledging of the house for conducting Usha's marriage and also promised that he would send us the money shortly for redeeming the house. Once again I lent father a sum of Rs. 18,000/- towards the processing fee for the loan application of pledging the house. The house was pledged and an amount of Rs. 1. 5 lakhs was received by father from the bank.

In the meanwhile, we received a letter from Babu, in which he had informed us about his desire to find a new job in Jamaica and about his obtaining an extension of stay in that country after seeking permission from the Immigration Authorities.

Hope things are quite all right over there. Its really a long time since I had thought of writing to you. Since I had planned to come over during the end of May 1997, I thought, let me give some rest to my ink and paper. Well, things have worked out different now. I am expecting a job closer to the United States. But you know the processing time and the procedures take a whole lot of time. I am prepared to wait till things fall my way. The Lord had put me under severe test and I know it was all for a purpose. You should quite understand that if I come back to India and try for a job overseas, it is going to be very difficult. Competition is obviously more in India. You would surely agree with that. Now, I have been applying to many countries, I hope I get a job in countries like Canada, Belize, US or Cayman Islands. I had gone to the Immigration Department and convinced them and got an extension of stay in the country. In fact I did this so as to save the money and transfer it to you. Any how, I really felt bad when I received a letter stating that the house was going to be pledged. I really feel sorry about the inability of either of you in running things. One thing you should understand is that it is very easy to borrow. I really thank the lord that till date I had not met with a situation where I should borrow money from "Tom, Dick or Harry". Neither the Credit Union nor the banks. Well, it has been a struggle but you know that's how life is. Running from "pillar to post" or "hand to mouth" is a common thing for us middle class people. I envy people who prosper. I envy my colleagues who make money easily. But well, I convince myself stating that the lord has not looked on "Us" as yet. But well, might be he is testing us. Might be we would prosper more than the people whom we envy. Its just a matter of time. Well, if we can wait and bear the pains, and trust in the "Almighty" with true faith, we are sure to prosper. Well, I don't want to become a millionaire overnight. I have a goal and the goal is to reach a stage for me to have things that I need in life, to buy things what my brothers, sisters, father, mother and relatives need; immaterial of the cost of material or item. I consider myself to be a good philanthropist.

Well, I love to help people, I love to work / service goods free of cost just to have a good name in my community, but well, I have not reached that stage as yet. I need money and have to work hard for it. The lord I am sure will bless all my ambitions if my faith is real. I would reach my goal but well its for you all to have the patience. Well, I spoke to Raghu and father alone the other day. Sorry, I could not speak to anyone else. Well, let me tell you the story. I bought a telephone, international / world tele card for 575 J$. In fact, I never knew the cost of telephone had increased. I was of the view that I can speak for at-least 5-6 minutes. But I could not believe the line got cut within two minutes. Well, I know I am really not aware of what is going on with the country. I hardly watch the television or hear the news on radio. Well, the lord always keeps me busy. Work has kept me going. Good thing I have a trade. I thank father for having put me in the right trade. I do make money. To be frank, I have worked for more than half a million dollars so far, during my two years. But the fucking cost in this country is so high that you make money and then you end up spending the same.

It has been hard to save. I have of-course been saving. Well, you think why this guy's handwriting is bad and also if I am mad. Well, I am mad. I am in fact writing this letter from one of my client's office. She has asked me to wait. But for how long ? Its two months already. 45,000 J$ is due from her. Can't wait any longer. Do or die! Today I want to finalise. If she feels she is big, I am much more bigger with the faith I have on the lord. You think I am joking. No, I am serious, I want my money. This lady is on tour for a couple of weeks, come when she feels like and when she leaves, no one knows when she is coming back. She is here today and I hope I see her and get my money. Not a big amount. You know 45,000 J$ is just a little pocket money. But this money in India is really big money.

I am going to transfer a bit of money to you. Rupees One lakh. Now, tell me what you are going to do with this money ? I want to really know. I had some bad experience with you people spending my hard earned money in a stupid way. Now, although I had told Raghu and father that I am sending money during the first week of June, I really want to know if my money is going to be spent usefully. Well, I don't want to embarrass you people. I want my hard earned money to be spent usefully. Please write to me immediately on what you plan to do. Well, if I am convinced, I am bound to help you out. Please don't mention the ridiculous expenses of Raghu's card business or grocery expenses.

I am continuing my letter after another two hours. I am sort of hungry. But still waiting on the fucking lady to talk to me. Looks like she is still busy. But well, that's how I am gaining experience in having patience. I am prepared to wait for the next two hours. But need to see her and get my money.

Well, what next to write, I have no idea. How is Vinu doing at school ? I really would like to see her latest photograph and all of yours. I don't know if I can make it during September 1997. I probably wish to come over, spend a couple of months and then return back to wherever God has destined me to go. I am really fed up. Is it because I have been waiting for so long or is it some sort of frustration in me, I really can't understand. (Well, looks like the long stupid / idiotic meeting is done, I hope I get to speak to this fucking woman and go home and have some good food and rest). You know one of the wickedest thing in this world that I do not like is the waiting.

Well, I am not really convinced with the meeting that I had and neither did I get the money. Well, people consider me to be a money man. In fact they call me "money man", millionaire,. . . . . But only the lord knows about the money that I would hardly have in my pocket. May be I / we should stop complaining about things. The lord may take away our blessings. We are really not happy with what the lord has given to us. We should thank the lord for what he has given.

Compare those with less fortune than us. Anyhow I am boring you people.

Well, I don't know, I look at things at all angles and with my faith I think I am doing things the right way. I don't know when I would be coming. I am so moody that I may plan a short trip before I start my new endeavour. Well, that's it for now. I just would wait to get a detailed letter from you on how you would be spending the money. On receipt of the same, I would send the money. Also, write to me about mother's health.

Father was happy to note that Babu would be sending rupees one lakh shortly and he wished to repay the bank loan which he had obtained for conducting Usha's marriage. Mother was admitted in hospital for a minor foot surgery. During Usha's marriage, she was unable to move around and quietly sat on a chair with her legs stretched out in front of her. More than the pain in her foot, mother was worried about Usha leaving the family. Usha had all along taken care of the family with great love and care and now mother felt crippled at the thought of missing her. She wondered how she was going to run the family without her help!

31

No Money to Buy Air Tickets

Raghu was adding up father's tension day after day. He was unable to pay up his dues to the people from whom he had borrowed money. Very soon, they were coercing him to repay their loans. However, Raghu was cool and he kept dodging them. Finally when they started coming home, he was neither available at home or would direct them to meet father. Father would then pacify these men by telling them that his elder son was in Jamaica and had promised to send money shortly. When he received the same, he would pay their dues fully.

As promised, Babu sent rupees one lakh to father. However, father could not use the money for redeeming the mortgaged house. Bombarded with financial pressure from the debtors from whom Raghu had borrowed money, he had to part with the money to repay Raghu's loans. Little did he realize that by doing so, he had committed a great blunder in his life.

Father pretty well knew that it was not fair on his part to expect any money from Babu in the offing. With no financial help from Babu, father was forced to use his entire pension for household expenses. Now father worried about the housing loan which kept mounting.

Having sent up all his savings to help father in redeeming the house, Babu was left penniless. In the following letter, he describes about his trials with regard to finding a new job in order to earn some money to purchase his air-tickets and return to India.

Its really a long time since, I had thought of writing to you, but things had kept me busy and engaged. I had been traveling around the country seeking contracts. Things are not bright and are very slow. Unfortunately, the finance situation presently with me is too bad. The money that I had for my "air tickets" has diminished almost to nothing. I am really working harder so that I could be financially secured. I was also happy to note that Usha's marriage was performed grandly.

I am presently trying to save money for my air-tickets. Once I make the money, I would like to return back to India and try a job in the Gulf. In the meantime, if prospects change here, I would keep you informed. I am really not sure of when I would be reaching India.

Let me tell you something. I got a job in Belize (North America) as a Resident Services Engineer. But, I was unfortunate. They had given me one weeks' time to join. I never realized that I would have such technical difficulties. Can you imagine. The air-tickets were sent to me, money in advance was sent to the airport. A car had also been sent at the airport. Well, all travel arrangements were made by the company.

Now, I communicate with them the day on which I would be landing there. Since the tickets were "Open", my passport states I can travel to any country except South Africa. So I had taken it for granted that I would not have any problem with the Immigration.

I was shocked when the Immigration authorities told me I cannot fly as my passport does not have a VISA. Well, my arguments were in-vain. I lost my cool ; rather I was depressed.

I called my employer and he gave me some more time to look after all legal requirements. I did a stupid thing and I regret for it. I could have traveled through "PANAMA". But my presence of mind just failed. Well the unfortunate thing is that I could not travel. I lost the opportunity, rather a golden opportunity.

Well, I only hope things would change and may be I would get a better opportunity. I really don't know what is wrong with me. There was a time that so many companies wanted me and now is a time when nobody even corresponds to my applications. Well, people say that the economy of the country is going from bad to worse. The price of every little thing is going up. Saving becomes difficult. The more you save, the more you end up in spending. I tell myself I want to come out of Jamaica and go to some other island. But when is it going to happen, I ask myself. I keep trying and just have been getting negative responses. I sometimes get fed up and am right now fed up. I only wished I had a Bachelor's degree. I sometimes feel like joining the college. But the fees is too high. Books are expensive. The minimum cost of a book varies between J$ 3000 to J$ 4000. Can you imagine the college fee. I just have to forget about doing any course at all. Well, I have been boring you telling my story.

How are things at home ? How is Vinu doing at school ? How is mother's health. I would also like to get more details about Usha's marriage. How is Ramesh doing ? Is he still working in the same company. I only wish he still continues. I really do know the difficulties that father would be undergoing. I am sorry that presently I cannot do any thing to help him out of the finance situation. I only hope he can manage the crisis.

My plan right now is to save the money for my air-tickets. The fare is really expensive. Once I make the money, I would be coming straight back to India. But in the meantime, if something works out in terms of prospects in some other island, may be I would take a change.

Well, I know you people expect me to write frequently. But I don't know if I am lazy or if I don't have the time. Any how, I shall write more in my next letter.

Babu did not keep up his word. Probably, after sending us all the money he had with him, he had lost interest in the family. He did not phone up to us nor did he reply to father's letters.

On the other hand, Raghu enjoyed his life. He was now free from debts. Very soon, he found a new job and was crazy about a girl working there. He fell in love with her and this kept his mind off from the family. One day he revealed this to my parents and after getting their consent married her. Since, his wife and my mother could not get on well, he grumbled to me and sought my advice. I suggested him to move out of the house and he immediately obliged. He started constructing the first floor ; once again taking loans from banks. However, this time, he did not disturb father in any way. With a family of his own, his relationship with all of us slowly dwindled and he had never been of any financial help to father.

32

The Boss is Always Right

Now that Usha's marriage was over, I decided to have my second child. The morning sickness and other health related problems kept my mind off from my family. I really could not bother much about the difficulties encountered by father with regard to running the family. Nor was I concerned about the enhancing housing loan. Father however remained cool and confident. He believed that Babu would one day get settled in his life and start sending money to redeem the house. Unmindful of the fact that his letters remained unanswered, father continued to write to Babu every month.

One fine day, after almost an year, when the postman handed over an Air Mail envelope to us, we were so thrilled. I anxiously tore open the letter and started to read voraciously:

Its really a long time since we had communicated with each other. Well ,things have been rough from my end as well as your end. I am really sorry that I never corresponded to you people for almost a year. The money that I saved was used to buy some tools for my workshop. My workshop business is sort of slow presently. Money flow into my workshop became almost nil. People began to owe me. You would not believe if I tell you that about a 100,000 dollars are outstanding towards the works that I have done for people.

I am looking for a job presently with the lessons that I have learnt. I have been without a job for almost eight months. My little saving keeps me going. My workshop does not do well either. I plan to come back to India. But how ? Money is the problem. That is the reason why I never wrote to you nor called you over phone. I want you to bear with me and pray for me. If I get a job for even a year, I am sure I can clear all the debts, save for my air-tickets and return for my better endeavours to India. I was promised a job by the end of this month. I am not sure how it is going to be. Well, I know all these burdens on me are just because of my foolishness. I feel for it now. I should have never left India in the first place. I would have been better off with the work I had in Gremach Limited. Even otherwise, I could have settled my life as a lecturer in Pondicherry. Well, past is past and I know things for me over here are not going to stay the same way. I only need your blessings and prayers.

I always wonder, why from the first day I had been in Jamaica, till now, I am facing hardships. I don't know what is wrong with me. I had a couple of good jobs. My superiority complex made me just kick off those and well, I regret now. Its too late, but better late than never. I have realized that the boss is always right. There's no use of arguing with him. Anyhow, I am totally a changed man now. Any work I get, I would leave only for one reason - either better prospects or returning back to India.

My address remains the same. Once I get through with my work, I can assure you that I would call you more frequently. Till such time, you have to really cooperate with me.

Convey my best wishes to every one in the family. I will write to you every thing in detail after I get my work. I am only sorry that I cannot clear all your debts till I get some work.

Please send a family photograph if possible. Please send Sai Baba's 'vibhuthi' along with a photograph.

As I finished reading the letter, my excitement slackened and I became downhearted. Babu still continued to lead a miserable life. And if at all there was any positive note in it, it was the fact that Babu had learnt his lesson in his life; the hard way. He realized that his present condition was his own doing. He repented for his past actions and I felt happy that hence forth he would change for the better.

33

The Baby Sitter

On 22nd October 1998, God blessed me with a son, whom we named as Tarun Sekar. The caesarian was a complicated one this time ; resulting in a lot of blood loss. All of a sudden, my BP and pulse became low and only after giving me three bottles of blood, my health showed signs of improvement. It was due to the doctor's constant vigil and monitoring, that I returned to normalcy. And when at last I came out of anesthesia, I held on to my father's hand and cried. It was a revival of my life with God's blessings! That instant, my thoughts turned to my brother Babu. I missed him a lot and how I wished, he was there by my side to see my little son.

My mother came to stay with us to take care of the baby. She had a tough time indeed! For my daughter Vinodhini who was six years old was filled with pangs of jealousy whenever she saw her grandmother and her little brother together. One day, when she returned from school, she saw her grandmother with the baby on her lap. She became so wild and yelled at her, "throw him down first!" My mother, immediately obliged for she did not wish to confront her tantrums and put the baby on the bed. Vinu then jumped and sat on her lap. Mother could not stay with us for long. For, she had to take care of my sister, who was in her last leg of pregnancy.

I then had to engaged a live-in servant to take care of my son. While I was away to office, father came home everyday to baby sit my children. I did not wish to leave my children under the care of a servant maid. And when I returned home in the evening, father would give me a gist of the activities of my two naughty children. Later on, at the time of leaving, he would grumble about two things. One was his desire to see Babu, whose whereabouts we were not aware of and the other was the housing loan which had mounted to rupees two lakhs.

34

Stranded in a Foreign Land

While I really could not offer any help in redeeming the house, I decided to do something about tracing the whereabouts of Babu. I was actually awestruck by the fact that Babu had not spoken to us for nearly two years now. Whenever, I booked a call to Jamaica, I received the same answer from the operator – "There is no response or Sampath has left the place". This time I was bent upon talking to him, unmindful of the expenses involved. After booking an ISD call, I waited with abated breath. When at last the call came through, I doubled over and picked up the-phone. A lady with a sweet voice informed me to stay on the line while she was trying to connect me to Jamaica. After a short while, the operator came on the line with the same negative answer, "someone is telling me that Sampath has left the place. " I then pleaded with the operator to enquire the speaker if Sampath had left behind his contact number. She obliged and within a few seconds came back on the line with a new contact number. I thanked her profusely for her help and once again requested her to try the new number. This time, she successfully connected me to Babu and on hearing my voice, Babu was appalled. "How did you get this number?" He asked with amazement. I explained everything to him and finally before disconnecting, he gave me his cell phone number and told me to contact him in that number henceforth. He also promised to write a detailed letter shortly. The fact that Babu could now be contacted whenever we intended to, filled me with great joy and confidence.

When Babu's letter reached us, I tore open the letter in a great hurry and started reading the same curiously. I was longing to know about Babu's present life in Jamaica......

Its really a long time since I had written to you. I tried to call a couple of times but could not get connected. How are you all ? Hope things are prosperous with the family. I know you people would be disappointed with the way I treat you, but I cannot do any better. Things have become so difficult that I am running from pillar to post. My workshop was doing so good and I really could save money a couple of years before. But, now I am struggling. I don't know if there is any spell on me. I keep praying everyday. I don't have any money in the bank. What ever little money I make is spent on daily expenses. I don't have any good friend from whom I could seek a loan, to start over my life all over. I beg god to make an opening for me. Things have become rough in Jamaica. Cost of living is so high. I cannot sleep sometimes at nights. I wonder where the next dollar is going to come from. I am planning to find a different, fast going location to have my workshop. I used to ask myself this question "what am I going to be five years from now". But I have changed that question. I ask myself "what am I going to be one month from now". Its hard. I should accept the fact that I took a wrong decision in my life ; to leave INDIA. Well, I love to come back. But how ? Dollar 138,000 is the air fare. That is big money for me now. I am really sorry that I miss all of you. I am waiting for God to make my dream come true. I want to make some money and leave Jamaica.

I know that something is wrong with me. I do know that there is a bad spell on me. I keep praying and I know God is *with me. I got a very good contract with a tourist resort. I got a pay of 40,000 dollars every month, with free boarding and lodging. Everything was free. I did save money. But the hotel was forced to lay me off as their business became slow. They could not afford to have me. I left them on good terms. The money that I saved was used to open a bar. I did make money. Suddenly, things totally changed. Business became slow. All my savings had to be drawn for food. My saving account is presently having $80/-. Its about six months since I have gone to the bank. I feel ashamed of even facing the bank officials. They have always rated me as a person who holds money. When I broke the fixed account, the bank manager (a friend of mine) asked me, what really is wrong with me. I had to tell her a lie saying, I am going back to INDIA. Till date, I have no transaction with them. A couple of weeks before, I made about a 20,000 dollars. I thought of depositing at least 10,000 dollars. Looks like the devil heard this. There was immediate expense for the entire money. I thought it was for good. But it turned out to be a big disappointment. Let me tell you the story. It was a big job with the government of Jamaica. During June 2000 I saw an advertisement in the newspaper seeking "maintenance officer". I applied and got a prompt answer. I went for the interview spending about $5000. They were very happy and said I would have to go to the Head office for a final interview. I spent about $3500. They were happy and asked me when I would join. Well, I was waiting for the "offer letter". They had promised to send the letter in one week's time. Almost every day, I was in the post office. One week passed and the second. . . . . Till, one day during the third week, I received their response. I was so happy. I was telling myself, at-last I think I have settled in a proper job. I already had plans of what I am going to do with the gross pay of $600,000 per annum. I was so excited that I never wanted to pull out the letter in the post office. I reached home as early as possible, and with great joy, I pulled out the letter from the envelope. It read as follows :*

"Dear Mr. Kumar,

After careful observation and analysis of your interviews, we regret that we cannot offer you a job now. Thank you for your efforts. We wish you all the best in your endeavours. "

I cried to myself. What did I do to deserve this treatment. Why is God so bitter with me. I took nearly two weeks to forget the entire episode. Things began to get stiffer and stiffer. Harder and harder. One afternoon, during September, lying on my bed, I took the "Bible" put it on my chest and spoke to God. "God, if you claim you are powerful, if you claim you are great and almighty, perform a miracle in my life. I give you three days time to accomplish this"

I felt some spirit moving in me and it said, "Son, you don't have to wait for three days, I am going to do it now".

I jumped out of my bed. Was I dreaming ? No, I was very well conscious. My whole body was like a feather. I knew God had touched me. I put the Bible in the corner of my bed and went outside by the verandah and sat in a chair, just confused. Couple of minutes later, a car stopped right in front of the house and delivered a note. "Immediate. . . . . call. . . . . "

My Goodness, can you imagine. After 3 months, the same government agency wanted me. I called them and they asked me if I am still interested. I said yes and was in great joy. I began to go all over and tell them on how God had touched me and performed to me this miracle. I was to join them in a couple of weeks. I began to pack up. I told all of my friends that they would not see me again. "God has opened a door for me and nobody can shut it". I was showing off. Showing off the power of God. What God can do and how great he is.

Alas! A couple of days after, a call again. A little confusion. They want copies of all my testimonials. I was asked to reach back. Can you imagine, an extra $5000/- expenses. I was upset. I could not tell them I had no money. I had to raise my voice. I called the two places, Hotel and the head office and told them if they never had a look on the certificates during the interview. Talking to the General Manager, I got the consent just to courier the whole package. I still had to spend about $2000. I was glad it reached them. One hell again. A couple of days later, another call. "Oh, Mr. Kumar, we are sorry. There is one form that you need to fill out". I lost my temper. I was to travel about 120 miles (5 hours journey). No, I asked them if they could fax it to me. The answer was "No". I have to reach there and fill it up. Expenses again. I made it clear to the General Manager, if he was now sure of all the documents. I asked him twice before I left. He said yes and the appointment order would reach in by Thursday. My foot! A call on Monday again stating the reference number is missing. I just raised my voice and asked the woman if she could not check it out with the "Directory Assistance". I told her very clearly that she is the one that is purposely giving me all these trouble for nothing. Well, I went home upset but was confident that everything would be all right by Thursday. I kept telling myself, "seek the kingdom of God first and everything shall follow. When God opens a door for you, nobody can shut it".

Tuesday Morning, a call again. "We cannot get proper references, Mr. Kumar". The concerned referees have left Jamaica for a vacation and one reference says she does not know much about you. I called back that reference and asked her if she does not know me. "Yes Sam, I do know you. You used to service air-conditioners for about two years. But the woman is asking me questions like, 5 years from now, how do you rate SAM. . . . . etc. which I cannot answer".

I called back the bitch, the woman, and yelled at her. I spoke to the boss and explained everything that happened from

June 2000 till the day. I told him, on how this woman is giving me all kinds of complications. I told him very clearly that, it was they who called me and why all this confusion. "I just want a "Yes" or "No" answer. I told them I would call them next day morning by 10.00 a.m. I never bothered to call them neither did they.

It took two weeks for me to cool down. But I began to ponder "when god opens a door, nobody can shut it". Yes it is true. But I think I shut it by myself and I am the cause. Nobody is to blame. I still have my faith and am confident that I would get a response from them. I keep praying and do know it is going to be answered as early as possible.

Incidentally there is a next job that I am negotiating. I went there yesterday (2nd October). I am to go there again on the 5th. I wonder how it is going to turn out. The last $1000 that I had was spent for this purpose. This morning, I woke up with just 2000 $, all in my name. Electricity bill amounts to $3400. Due date is the 21.9.2000. Today is the 3. 10. 2000. Are they going to disconnect supply ? I don't know. That would be a big embarrassment. To reconnect, with penalty would cost about $10,000. I am confused. No money and with no power, my little means of income from the workshop is going to be doomed. Well, I called them, let them know "not to disconnect and give me time till Friday" Hopefully, God would not put me into any embarrassment.

I need a job. I need to go into a different fast going parish. I need to make some money. I need to leave Jamaica.

I am sorry, I have been telling my story and never asked anything about you people. I want you to write to me at-least once in a month. I have nobody here and God is my only friend. I think he makes me go through all these tribulations for a reason. I know I am going to win.

How is mother ? How is father ? How are the little ones. How is Raghu's wife ? I want you to send me a picture of Usha and her husband with the kid, Hema and Gnanasekar with the kids, Raghu and his wife with the little one. How is Ramesh doing ? Has the house loan settled ?

Hema - a special request

(1) Pray for me. Is there any special puja you can do to clear the spell on me ? Send me a silver ring of SAIBABA and a silver chain with SAIBABA on it. I think it would change my life with blessings. The manthras of SAI BABA ; I would like to have a copy of them.

(2) Also look at my horoscope. Check it out with a good astrologer. Send me the details of it.

I love to come home for Deepavalli 2000. Will I make the money by that time ? Lets wait and see.

Hema, You know that your faith is really strong. I always look on the miracles that God had performed in your life. Just writing to you, I tell you although I closed my letter, I can't stop writing. An envelope addressed to the house was delivered. The contents do not correspond to me. But there was US $20 in it. i.e. Jamaican dollars J$ 800. Don't you think that was a great blessing. God is really great. The letter was to be delivered to someone, somewhere. But it reached me. I need it and I know it is God who sent it to me. I think, I am getting more matured in terms of love towards God. Incidentally a couple of hours later, a woman who owes some money for me for a very long time had come and cleared her bill of $500. Further, there are two fridges that I have been called to service. What a blessing. Thank God for what He is doing. I know my electricity is not going to be disconnected. My faith is strong in the Lord. Look, one of my friends from a different parish has come and wants me to start the business over there. Rent $1000 monthly. He says enough *people want my services. Can you imagine three miracles since I closed the letter. Praises to the Almighty, our lord, the great.*

Are Raghu and Ramesh taking proper care of mother and father. I love them so much. I don't want anybody to disgrace them. If I come down and hear any hard feelings my mom and dad have for any body, you know I am damn serious guy. Are Raghu and his wife all right. Behaving good with mother and father. Tell father to have more faith and courage and nobody to frighten him with anything. The land is his and the house is his. Well, you know they are getting old and ask them not to take any foolish decisions. I love my mother. Its a pity that I can't see her. But, one thing I know you are taking 100 % care of her. How is her B. P ? I don't want her legs to be amputated at any cost. If that happens, you are responsible. I will never have a word with you till the end of my life. Take care of father. How is his eye sight ? I long to see him. Sometimes, in the nights, I cry to myself. You know we have the best daddy and mommy in the world. They would do anything for us. I remember how father cried when he left me in Dindigul college. I remember how mother used to always help me with her little hard saved money. I love the little girl "Vinu". I hope she is doing well with everything. I sometimes look on her picture and tell her, "little girl, your uncle will soon see you". I sent back message through every flight I see.

How is my bike ? How are my tools ? How are the three suitcases that I had locked and left over the loft. Who takes care of all the photographs I had left there. Is my Name plate still at the front of the house (S. Sampathkumar, AC & Refrigeration Engineer). How does the house look like ? Can you send me a picture of it ?

How is Usha ? I hope she is happy. She has helped us so much that I know God would have blessed her with everything in her life. My sisters are thousand times better than gold.

Hema, I am going to end this note. Please write to me everything in detail and send me what I have asked you to send. I hope God would be with us in all our endeavours and make us prosperous.

Hope Ramesh is still in the job and upgraded himself. He should be saving money by now.

As I finished reading the letter, all my excitement languished. Babu had still not settled in his life. He was so desperate to find a new job and earn money to return to India but however all his attempts in finding one were meeting with failure. His helplessness changed him into a God fearing person and his faith in Him suddenly snowballed. He turned to God for succor.

Babu had indeed portrayed a very dismal picture of the life he was leading in Jamaica. He was in fact stranded in a foreign land and could not return to India and neither could he be of any financial help to the family. My spirits fell low and I became downcast. I folded the letter with a heavy heart!

35

Overwhelmed by a Sharp Feeling of Guilt

I was aggrieved by the sad plight into which Babu had landed himself in. A sharp feeling of guilt overwhelmed me. In fact, I had been indirectly responsible for Babu's present predicament. If only, I had not coaxed him to go abroad to earn money, things would have been smooth both in the family as well as for Babu. Out of love I had for father and with the sole aim of turning my family rich, I had joined father in persuading Babu to leave the country. Babu was now in a quagmire. He was neither having sufficient funds to purchase his air-tickets and return to India, nor was he able to offer any financial help to father.

Mother was also depressed about Babu's ordeals. She became tensed and worried a lot about him. As a result of this, her blood sugar refused to come down despite taking insulin injections everyday. Her different parts of the body were also affected due to this. Once, a small swelling erupted on her spinal column. She was admitted in the hospital and a surgery was done. When the doctor himself informed us that it was a serious case, I began to panic. What if mother passed away without seeing Babu! She had all the while been waiting to see her son. If something untoward happened to her, I shall then never die in peace. I offered nonstop prayers to God and slowly mother recovered miraculously. She stayed in the hospital for almost two months for treatment of her carbuncle back.

Father had been lingering around with a gloomy face for quite some time now. I thought that the reason for this could be his helplessness in bringing Babu back to India. However the truth dawned on me very soon. One evening, when I returned from office, father was rather unusually morose and did not even talk to me. He did not even offer his usual complaints about my children, which he would normally do. Before leaving, he pulled out a letter from an registered cover and handed it over to me. The letter was from the bank, intimating that if the loan amount of Rs. 2.3 lakhs was not paid within a period of one month, the house would be put up for auction. So, this was the reason for father's glumness. I was really shocked and became dumbfounded.

36

A Wild Goose Chase

Ever-since I heard from father that the house was going to be put up for auction, I lost my sleep. I was breaking my head as to how best I could be of help to father in redeeming the house. Babu, the only source of help known to me was himself stranded in a foreign land. Raghu had his own family to take care of and hardly was concerned about the gravity of the situation. Night and day, I was dwelling upon the best possible way by which I could help father tide over the financial crisis in redeeming the house. I kept brooding over the fact that if no one was willing to help father, very soon, my old parents would find themselves on the streets. And I had to do something and act fast too.

It was during this time that my mind became crazy and got distracted from the routine of life. I was possessed with a mania. Once again, it was my father who initiated the nonsensical and absurd fad into my life. One evening he phoned up to me and said, "There is an interesting quiz programme on TV, hosted by the famous Hindi actor Amitabh Bachchan. The questions are so simple and with your excellent general knowledge, you can give it a try!"

The programme he referred to was *Kaun Banega Crorepati* (KBC). The quiz game show had fifteen multiple choice questions, and one who answered them all correctly was rewarded with a cash prize of rupees one crore! Of course one had also the benefit of three lifelines to seek help from, when one was not sure of the answer. Well, once again it was money that father was after. I told him that I really did not have the time for it and I was not interested.

However, he kept reminding me about the programme quite often and urged me to give it a try. One day, I went to my parents' home with my children. After spending some time with us, father went inside saying "I have got a gift for you. " He returned with a small package inside which was a quiz book meant specially for this programme. I just scanned through the pages and suddenly my interest in the programme was aroused. I decided to give it a try for a trial costs nothing. Thus began a mega project!

I talked it over with my husband and convinced him that if I had to take part in the KBC show, his cooperation was the most important thing. First of all he would have to let me watch the programme from 9 p.m. to 10 p.m. everyday. He should also let me prepare for it, without grumbling. He gave his consent immediately! I then assured him that, I would pray to God whole-heartedly and try my best to win the Rs. one crore-prize money, which he could spend as he liked.

.........After redeeming the house for father and bringing my brother back to India, I would take my family on a world tour! I would travel by executive class and sit amidst rich businessmen, famous actors and reputed politicians! Looking at me, they would first wonder as to who this ordinary woman was. Slowly my face would appear a little familiar. Then they would recall everything. Yes! This was the intelligent woman, who answered all the questions on the Big B's game show! And

they would think how true it is said that beauty and brains don't always go together. Very soon they would all start staring at me and wish to have a conversation with me. Oh! God, at that time, please make me feel humble and do not let pride or ego take over me!. . . . . .

The summer vacations had begun and I was spared from school work. Having time on my hands, I decided to take the plunge. The preparations began in earnest. My mind was always preoccupied with what I had to read and what reference books I had to buy. One morning, while going up to my office, I was so engrossed in my study plan, that I continued climbing till the fourth floor. When I realized my mistake, I turned back and walked down to the third floor, where my office was. I felt like a schoolgirl once again filled with dread - as though everything depended on my passing the exam!

I purchased a general knowledge book for rupees twenty from a bookstall at the railway station followed by a hefty *Competition Success Review*. Then, I jotted down important points from it. I requested father to buy some more quiz books and very soon the table was piled high with reference books. I had almost spent a thousand rupees towards purchase of quiz books by various authors. I worried a lot that I had very little time to prepare and felt that had I been a housewife, things would have been much easier!

I watched the quiz programme and found that the pattern of questions varied everyday and they were set and based on the participant who was sitting on the "hot seat", his qualifications, nature of work, the politics and history of the place to which he belonged, his religion, language, culture, and so on.

Hence, I subscribed to the magazine, *India Today* to have a fair knowledge of Indian politics. From the library, I borrowed the historical and religious comics, and read them over and over again. One day, I picked up about ten comics, and the librarian stared at me in great awe. I told him that I was taking it for some reference study and would return them within two days. I did not want to brag to him that it was for the KBC show, and wished to keep it a secret. *When he watches me on the TV quiz programme he will probably think, well it was for this, that the lady had taken all the books that day!*

My hands hurt as I jotted down the points from each and every reference book in front of me. Finally, the notes I gleaned almost became another thick book! I also realized that whatever I crammed from these books, I forgot the next instant. Preparing for the show was becoming too much of a bother and I was also filled with confusion of what exactly I ought to do. Then it occurred to me that my own preparations were not going to be helpful and God's blessing was all that mattered. I wrote the names of all the quiz books on different bits of paper and shuffled them in front of God. I then prayed to Him, "Oh God! Only you are aware of all the questions that I will be asked on the game show. Now, tell me the one and only book from this lot, which will help me achieve my goal!" Closing my eyes, I picked up a chit and to my astonishment, it was the very first book which I had purchased from the railway bookstall for just rupees twenty. Had I known it before, I could have avoided buying the other books and saved a lot of money!

The next day, I wrapped up all the quiz books together and placed them on a glass bookshelf. But whenever I went past the bookshelf I felt rather guilty. I had spent so much on these books and now they were gathering dust! However, I had taken a firm stand and didn't wish to muddle through these books again. I pulled out the package from the bookshelf and hurled it as far as I could into the loft where it would not be visible and from where it could not be easily brought down. I consoled myself that one day these books might be useful to my children and it was not a sheer waste of money, after all!

Day in and day out, I crammed the questions from the one and only quiz book selected by Him. Very soon, I was familiar with almost all the questions in it! Everyday, I would sit on the floor with a notebook and pen and jot down the questions appearing on the game show. My children were even too excited to watch the programme! Not that they understood anything, but they were happy to see how animated their mom got when she knew the answer to any of the questions. Also, they were thrilled to see their mother sit in one place for such a long time. My daughter would prop herself against me and my three-year-old son would lie on my lap, enjoying the closeness.

One fine day, Big B announced that the phone lines were all open and the participants who wished to take part in the game show could try their luck.

.... *Yes! I am going to try this time! Here I come, Mr Big B, to shake your hand and accompany you to the hot seat!* ....

I noted with diffidence that Mr B shook hands with women too (instead of saying namaskar, the usual Indian way of greeting others, by folding, the palms together). I would have to be courageous enough to shake hands with Big B! So, I was bent upon transforming my style and personality altogether. That weekend I went to a beauty parlour and got a U-shape haircut.

...........*On seeing me in the game show, the beautician will tell her assistant proudly, "This was the lady who came to our parlour a few weeks back!"* ....

I dialled the number till my hands ached and finally left the task to my daughter. She sat by the phone and patiently tried the number continuously. Within a few minutes she succeeded and I ran over to the phone, with my heart pounding.

A recorded voice said that I would first have to answer a multiple-choice question. Having not got over the excitement of getting the line, the question was neither audible nor clear to me. However, after evoking God's grace, I punched the answer. To my astonishment, the recorded voice said, "well done, your answer is right! Please stay by your phone on the eigtheenth, and we will let you know if you are one of the lucky participants. And if for some reason you are not available on that day, we will move on to the next lucky contestant. "

That night, while watching the programme, I became restless. One participant had answered all the fourteen questions correctly. He had to answer one more question to win the jackpot. Meanwhile, Big B was asking him what he intended to do with such a large sum. And the participant started bragging about his intentions. Suddenly, my imagination soared very high.

.... " Hemaji, could you please tell us what you intend to do with your prize money?"

"Well, actually it was my father, who coaxed me into taking part in this programme and I would like to redeem his mortgaged house, and one of my brothers has got stranded in a foreign land and I would like to help him come back and my sister..... " and the Big B would cut in sharply, "let us continue after a short commercial break", for the list was going to be endless! ....

On D-Day I pulled up a chair and sat down, beside the phone. The recorded voice had warned, "if you are not available on that day, we will move on to the next lucky contestant". So I made it a point to stay close to the phone all day. It was just before noon when all of a sudden, I felt like going to the toilet, but quickly changed my mind. What if the expected call came at that point of time, when I was answering nature's call! I continued with my studies and waited in vain, up to 6 p. m. When the call didn't come through by then, I was completely dejected.

But there was always a second chance and I tried the line once again, and this time too, I did not get selected. It was then that I lost all hope and my instinct warned me that the KBC show was a wild goose chase! For, to be a participant on this game show, what mattered was a great deal of luck and not just hard work. Thereafter, I did not wish to waste my time on an enterprise which depended primarily on chance. I would rather slog over some befitting venture, where hard work really brought its own fruits. My children's vacations had also come to an end, and once again there was a cartload of homework and monthly tests which I had to attend to. I resolved the KBC issue by covering the TV with a large cover, vowing never to open it again for a very long time. I abandoned the project in good earnest.

37

On the Valentine's Day

One midnight I was in deep slumber, when I got startled by the telephone bell. Babu was on the line and he told me that since it was a Valentine's Day, one could make calls across the globe free of cost in Jamaica. This time, he was in no hurry and spoke to me at length enquiring about mother's health. Suddenly, his voice became feeble and wobbly and he said, "Hem, I wish to confess something to you. But first promise me you won't reveal this to anyone!"

After I assured him that I would keep it a secret, he began, "Hem, I have been hiding a fact from all of you guys for the last four years. Actually, I am married and I also have a four year old daughter. Her name is Krishna Kumar and my wife's name is Maureen. " My head swirled and my eyes suffused with tears. It took some time for me to recover from the shocking news. I tried to maintain my cool. I did not wish to react in an adverse manner. For I feared that if I screamed at him or reproved him for betraying all of us, he would change his mind and never return to India. I shall then never become free from the guilt that I have been holding for long. Composing myself, I said "it is all right if you are married. There is nothing wrong in it. Our parents would tolerate their children and would not reproach you in any manner and so you must not hide this fact from them. " Finally, he agreed to tell them about this. "And now, tell me when are you going to come back to India ? Our parents are getting old and are longing to see you. All they ever talk of is about you. Please come back and after seeing them once, you can return back to Jamaica. We would happily welcome your wife and daughter and so please start immediately and come back to India. " My pleadings with him for his return to India continued for a long time.

And at last he said, "I shall come to India once I make the money to buy my air-tickets. " I was delighted to hear that Babu intended to come back to India after-all. And this filled me with momentary joy!

Suddenly, his speech turned jubilant and with an added vigour, he bragged, "Hem, my wife and daughter are by my side right now. Do you wish to speak to them?" I could not understand the accent of words Maureen uttered but I continued to speak to her. I actually wished to convey my thoughts to her and so I said, "please send Sampath to India. His parents are eager to see him. I promise to send him back to you!".

As I placed the phone on the cradle, I sat down and started brooding on the bleak future that was in store for us. All my expectations and dreams had got shattered. If at all there was an iota of hope in my mind that Babu would someday be of help in redeeming the house, it was gone now. He belonged to totally another world and I have no rights over him anymore. And this had been the reason for his missing letters and telephone calls and his altogether disappearing from our lives for a while ; until I tracked him down.

The next day, this was the topic of discussion among us siblings. We were sharing our views at the shocking revelation of Babu's marriage and his daughter. While talking to Raghu in this regard, he told me something about father, which set me off into a spell of laughter. You know something, he began, "while I was seriously talking to Babu about his marriage, father kept interrupting me relentlessly and requested me to find out from Babu when he would be sending us money. " Even a serious matter as his marriage was of no significance to father as much as his concern for money.

38

First Redeem the Mouse

The D-Day for the auction of the house was fast approaching. What upset me most was the fact that none of them were gravely concerned about the imminent crisis that we were to encounter and also were placid about its dire consequences. I could fathom the reasons for their unruffled behaviour. They were in fact confident that since I loved my parents so dearly they were pretty sure that I would not leave them in the lurch. This fact provoked me a lot.

Though outwardly father appeared to be cool and composed, he was in fact desperate. He was in a constant state of uneasiness. And he was also very badly longing to see his son. I felt sorry for my father who was of late behaving like a child. While he had lost all the hope that Babu would be of any help in redeeming the house, he was getting very anxious and worried and feared if he would ever see his beloved son or not. For one midnight he woke up all of a sudden, and started to wail and when mother questioned him, he said, "I very much long to see Babu. He is always in my mind now. I don't know if I will ever see him before my death. Mother told him not to worry and assured him that God would unite Babu with the family very soon. Early in the morning, when news of father's weeping reached me, I was too distressed. I immediately decided to talk to Babu regarding this.

That evening, I spoke to Babu and told him that father was too eager to see him and that he should somehow start and come to India very soon. However, I found that Babu was impassive to my pleadings and had taken the whole matter in a lighter vein. For, in order to confirm his date of return, when I asked him, when are you planning to come to India, he spoke to me in an insolent manner. " what for ? Where do you want me to stay when I come home ? On the streets ? First redeem the house and then let us talk about my coming home!"

The aversive and unsympathetic words of Babu traumatized me and I was overpowered by a deep feeling of guilt. What if my parents passed away without seeing their beloved son! If such a thing ever happens, I shall never die in peace. I was now bent upon bringing about a union between my parents and Babu. For this, first of all I had to redeem the house!

39

Don't Call Again

Since Babu had informed me point-blank that he would return to India only if the house was redeemed, I kept racking my brains day in and day out, as to how best I could help father in this endeavour. For if I do not intervene and redeem the house, I could never unite Babu with the family. For he threatened that he would not return to India until the house was redeemed. I shall then never be free from the guilt that I am holding. It was due to my coaxing that Babu left for Jamaica. However, things did not turn out as expected. Fate had dealt a severe blow to him as well as to us and my only aim in life presently is to bring back my brother to India and unite him with my parents. Till such time, I will not be able to sleep peacefully and my mind will always be filled with the guilt. Hence, I decided to do something and act fast.

The last resort as usual seemed to me that I should turn to my husband for assistance. I pleaded with him to support me one last time and promised him that I shall never disturb him again in life. Finally after several arguments and negotiations my husband reluctantly relented. He gave me permission to obtain loans from banks and he himself withdrew his entire PF amount. And finally, I was able to collect the required amount of Rs. 2.3 lakhs and the house was successfully redeemed.

Father was indeed thankful and happy with the enormous help that I rendered to him. However, he had something-else to grumble about now. Since he had to part with his entire pension money to enable me repay the loan that I had in turn borrowed from the bank, he was left penniless and was finding it very difficult to run the household. Though I helped him monetarily from time to time to buy the provisions etc, the electricity and telephone bills could not be paid in time and very often the connections were cut off for non payment of bills. Father kept his fingers crossed and still hoped that Babu would help him sooner or later.

Once, when Babu phoned up to mother, she briefed him about the acute money shortage that father was facing and told him that presently there was no power in the house. She wept while telling him this and requested him to send some money for footing the electricity bill. This outraged Babu immensely. After promising to help her, he immediately rang me up. He started to scream at me. "Hem", he said irately. "I really feel sorry at whatever is happening to my parents. And I am awfully ashamed that you are unmindful and least concerned about them. You have an AC, fridge, washing machine and all other modern amenities at home and you are enjoying a comfortable life. Are you not least bothered about the fact that my poor mother is suffering even without electricity at home. How will she sleep without a fan or where will she go if she wants to drink ice water..... his rantings continued until I could take it no longer and I had to forcibly interrupt him. "Babu, what nonsense are you talking ? You keep calling me selfish all the time. Is it not you who is actually selfish ? You left India with the sole aim of making our parents rich! But what did you do ? You had never cared for them. If I had not intervened, they would have come to the streets by now! On the other hand, you have got married and you are enjoying your life, unaware of whatever is happening down here. It is in fact you that is selfish and I really feel ashamed of you. Babu, listen now! You are never grateful to me for all the good I keep doing to our family. I am not interested to talk to you further and please don't call me again!"

As I placed the receiver on the cradle, I felt an acute sense of loss in my life. My eyes suffused with tears and my heart kept thudding against the ribs. I was suddenly overcome with a sense of anger combined with hatred towards my brother for the harsh manner in which he had spoken to me. For the next few days, I lingered around in a sulky and morose mood. Eventually, when I came out of my gloominess, I realized that more than the roughness exhibited by my brother, it was the bitter words spoken by me that kept tugging at my heart.

40

Playing a Double Game

Time assuages everything. The anger and hatred that I had for Babu for his rude words slowly left me. If there was one good thing that happened to me after the quarrel with Babu, it was the realization that dawned upon me. For the first time in my life, I lost all hope that Babu would ever be helpful to my family in bringing them out of poverty. If they were destined to lead such a life, no one can do anything about it. Frankly, now I did not care for his money. After-all, I did the best I could do, to save my family from coming to streets. I stopped looking forward to Babu's money!

It was mother who finally brought about a union between Babu and me. One weekend when I was with her, she received a phone call from Babu. While speaking to him, she said, "Babu, ever since you left home, it is your sister who has been taking care of all of us here. She has been footing all my medical bills and also redeemed the house for us, besides offering financial help from time to time. But for her, we would have been ruined by now. Please don't talk to her like that!" And with tears in her eyes, she pleaded that I speak a few words to him. I obliged. But this time, I did not talk to him about money. I just told him that our parents are getting old and if he did not make it soon, he will have to repent later ; for he will not be able to see them.

He assured me that once he saved sufficient funds to buy air tickets, he would leave Jamaica and that he himself was not sure when that would be. Here, father was facing acute shortage of money and this was turning him mad. He could not make both ends meet and the pecuniary condition of the family was getting on his nerves. He was like the crow which got stranded on a ship in the middle of the sea. Attempting to escape from there, it takes off and not finding any other source to rest upon, pathetically returns to the same ship. Father too was in a similar situation. Being very despondent. , a desire to seek any possible financial help from Babu was kindled in his mind once again. In good earnest, he requested me to write a strong letter and send it to Babu. I obliged him and drafted the following letter.

Dear Babu,

Hope this letter finds you and your family in good health and spirits. Actually, I am writing this letter, because father wanted me to write to you. On the Valentine's Day, when you had confessed the truth that you were married and had a daughter, I was really shocked. I think you might remember that, years back, when you had just landed in Jamaica, in one of my letters, I had asked you if you had got married, and you wrote back telling, I am writing nonsense. So, all these years, you had been playing a double game with us. I had also written to you, many a times, advising you to give up anger and ego, which would destroy a person's growth in life and you had not cared to heed to it. I have learnt one thing in life. Advising others is as bitter a pill to swallow, as it is for the one whom it is offered. So, I have, of late stopped interfering in other's life and taking decisions for them. Experience is the best teacher, and I am sure, all of them can learn their own lessons in this world. That's why, I did not want to write to you , in the first place but since father insisted me, I just wanted to please him and here I am writing this small note to you.

You had left India with the sole purpose of turning our family rich. And your parents and siblings had to undergo a pain, at the time of your parting. You may remember that your mother was lying in the hospital when you went to the airport. Unfortunately, it was your anger and superiority complex or the ego, which made you fight with your boss. Had you for a moment thought of your aged parents and the purpose for which you left India, you could have avoided an argument, no matter what, and continued your job with him and also attained the goal, for which you left your family. Unfortunately, as fate would have it, you had also not been also able to control your temptations of your age and had got married and also have a daughter. Now, I understand, that your character should have tremendously changed. Family life, you would have realized by now, is a committed life, where your anger or ego, when expressed in any form, would bring about its doom. I am atleast happy that now you have changed for the better, and with a daughter of your own, you would have understood by now, the pains your parents have all the while been undergoing from the moment you left, at the absence of their son.

Due to your hectic activities, perhaps you might have not had time, even to think of all of us, but we had all the time been thinking of you each and every moment of our lives so much so that, my little son, who had not even seen you, except in the photos, keeps asking me when will Babu mama come and what will he buy for me. When I tell him, he would buy you superb toys, his face would brighten up and he would start asking me the same question with an added vigor. Each time, I would tell him, the very same answer : he would be coming shortly, may be next month.

Father has asked me to convey this to you : Well, once again, it is about money that he had wanted me to write to you. In fact, you would understand as a father, what bringing up a child is all about. Imagine, how many hurdles he should have faced in life, bringing up five children, giving them the basic necessities of life, food, shelter, clothing and good education. You would understand the amount of sacrifices he had made in his life, in order to see his children shine in life. After my marriage, when I realized that I could not help my family like before, financially, I decided that you are the right person who could step into my shoes and that is why I had prayed so much and finally you landed up in Jamaica. But only, you had not taken my ambition and the purpose for which we painfully parted, quite seriously and had been self - centered and got carried away by your own life.

Well, that is the past and no use brooding over that now! Let me tell you the story of the present,. Since you had all the while been promising that you would send money and redeem the house or that you would come down and take care of everything, I had not bothered about the mortgaged house. It so happened that time flew very fast and one day there was a letter addressed to father from the bank, that if he did not pay Rs. 2,30,000/- (Rs. 1,50,000/- plus interests) within a month's time, the house would be put on auction. To tell you the truth, no one was bothered about this, and they were even planning to sell the house. But somehow, I could not bear to see father, at the time of disposing off his hard earned property, and so I took up this matter very seriously with my husband. Day in and day out, I prayed God to help me solve the problem. At last, my husband agreed to help me out. He gave me permission to obtain a loan from the bank. Now, since father is giving his whole pension to me every month, he is left with no money on hand. That day, when you phoned up and confessed about your marriage, all of us were horrified. But even on that day, while mother was talking to you, father was telling her to inform you to send money. Later, Raghu told me about this and I started laughing ; for a subject as serious as your marriage did not perturb him so much, as does his craze for money. Hope, at least now, you would think about him and of-course, with a little bit of sacrifice on your part, for you have a family of your own - try and help father monetarily and give him some peace of mind in his old age. (When you see your parents now, you would be startled, for both of them have lost their teeth).

I posted the letter after showing it to father. Father was anxiously looking forward to a positive response from Babu. He believed that Babu would at-least send him a little money to tide over his dire financial crisis. However, I was pretty sure that he was waiting in-vain.

41

Just One Square Meal a Day

I had indeed guessed right! For Babu did not offer even meager help to father. Rather he could not. He was not in a position to do any favour to father. For one night, he phoned up to me and pleaded like a child. "Hem, please help me! I am not having a single penny on hand. Just help me to leave Jamaica. Please send 500 US $ to me. I shall pack up and leave Jamaica for good, leaving everything behind me!". To me, his pleadings were merely a joke and I said, "Babu, "What is it you are talking about ?. Are you not aware of the fact that I had just helped father in redeeming the house. How do you expect me to send money to you now?"

"I promise to repay the whole money to you once I come back to India", he continued desperately, despite the clarification regarding my helpless-ness.

Not willing to give a discouraging reply to him I said, "I shall consider your request ; but not right away. I need sometime!"

The suffering he was undergoing presently in life was partly due to me and I felt obligated to help him return to

India. And so finally I said, "I shall pray for you! God will bless you and fulfill all your wishes!" However, there was no response from the other side. The phone had already got disconnected.

After that, Babu stopped speaking to us over phone. A year passed by quickly. The New Year Eve of 2002 began with hope as usual. I hoped that atleast this year, Babu should make it and return back to India. He had also forgotten to wish us for the new year and this worried us a lot. It was only during June that we received a letter from Babu. It was the most pathetic letter that we ever received from him so far. He had apprised us about the kind of life that he was leading now and how fate had been cruel with him and pushed him into brink of poverty resulting in his helplessness to take any decision in life.

Its seven years since I had left you all. I tried to make both ends meet, I think I tried my best but have failed in this endeavour. I could neither make you happy nor myself. Well, I believe these seven years are a punishment for me rather, prison life. Sometimes, I consider if these seven years of suffering is due to my stars or what you may call 7 ½ (Ellara Nattu Saniyan). Well, if it is so, I know I am bound to come out of this awful situation. I have had the hardest time, here in Jamaica. Everything I try to do ends up in failure. When I work for a company, I hardly can stay there for more than five months. It is like I am tied up somewhere. I cannot make a step forward. When I try, I am pushed back two steps backward. Sometimes, I curse god and ask if he really exists, or if he has any ears to listen. I did a grave mistake. I should not have left India. I should have joined some of the good jobs that were offered to me over there - Pondicherry (government), Thapar Group. . . . . I regret, but it is too late. "Better late than never". You people might think I am enjoying my life over here. To be truthful, you would never like to know. I am living on just "one square meal" for the day. It is almost an year since I have worked for any company. The business in my workshop is so poor. It is just a *hand to mouth situation. It is so hard to save. Everything is expensive. As you make some money, there is some expense. I am fed up. I am so used to problems and failure that, of late nothing really bothers me. To be frank with you, you know how long I wanted to write to you. My telephone has been disconnected, otherwise I would have been in touch with you often. I owe the company about 21,000 J$. They keep sending me the bills and I don't even pull them. I just tear them into two and put them in the garbage. I had to borrow this sheet of paper from a friend of mine. I don't even know, how I am going to post it or when I am going to post it. Its a good while, since I have touched a 500 J$ or a 1000 J$. It does not bother me. I have a credit with a shop and take whatever I need. When God feels sorry for me, one customer would come into my workshop and when I fix the fridge, I end up earning about 6000-7000 J$. This I have to pay to the shopkeeper. This is how it has been going on for one year. I consider myself as a brillant idiot rather than a damn fool. Otherwise, I would not have reached this state. I want to write everything in detail but I am afraid, the postage would add up. Needless to point that I have given up. It is a do or die situation. I have taken a very firm decision. I am in the process of getting a job in the capital city of Jamaica- Kingston.*

I am praying very seriously to the same god that I curse regularly. When I get this work, I want to save J$200,000 (i.e.) 4000 U$. I think I can make it in 4-5 months. 100,000J$ for my air-tickets, 50,000 J$ to start a business when I come to India, 50,000 J$ for my miscellaneous expenses in India.

However, I will leave some assets for my little daughter Krishna. I want to say good bye to Jamaica. I prefer to visit Jamaica once in every two years. When I reach India, I want to start my own service centre / workshop and in the meantime, I want to pursue my engineering - yes, B. E at Annamalai University (Part time). I regret so much leaving India and being tied up in poverty in Jamaica. Well, when I reach India and God makes it so happen that I get an overseas offer like Canada or Singapore, I might change my mind. But, this would be on a totally different contract. With my seven years of overseas experience, I would set the contract accordingly. If I don't get a job that would pay me to make all of us happy, I would rather struggle in Madras among all of you. I don't think my plan would fail. I have failed so many times. My master "FAILURE" is going to have mercy on me. Yes, I am positive to get a job by the end of June or early July. You know something, I used to be lucky all the while, when I used to offer "Vada Malai" to the Lord Anjaneyar - I don't even remember the place, its a couple of miles away from Tiruninravur. I am going to promise "Veer Anjaneyar" 13 vadamalas. I want to reach India by the end of November 2002. I want to be there for Diwali and to celebrate my birthday on the 4th of December with my offering to the temple. I know "HANUMAN" would just lift me from Jamaica and put me back in India like how He reunited RAM-SITA-LAKSHMAN in the history of Ramayana.

What if I should fail ? What if I don't end up getting the work ? I am being negative all of a sudden. I always like to think of how the negatives can be dealt with. It would be a shame if I have to bother any one of you. After seven years, so called overseas job and cannot even afford to buy the air-tickets. That is more than a disgrace. I pray this should not happen. I will write to you as soon as I get the job. If not, I would depend on Raghu. I think he has some influence with the travel agencies. He does not have to put himself in to debt. If he could get the air-tickets and 500 US$ and send it to me, I can promise him that when I reach India, I can clear the debt in 3-4 months.

The route he will have to book is as follows :

Montego Bay (Jamaica) - London - Bombay – Madras

This would be the last resort. Don't confirm dates till I communicate with you.

I am sure, I won't embarrass myself in making you people do the above favour. I am going to make my best attempts in securing the job and save the money and leave this island at the planned target.

I am confident that my plan would work. I keep telling this to myself. I am positive that even if my plans fail, Raghu would help me out. This is more than a crisis.

In fact, I am so serious of coming home and want Hema to type out an application and send out to various companies ; that when I land, it would be easier for me. Who knows , might be the company would even send my air-tickets if I sign a contract with them.

Hema, I would like you to type the application in a computer and send them to as many companies (hotels, hospitals, overseas). You may sign on my behalf. Might be I would be lucky with an overseas offer that it would be easier for the employer to recruit me from Jamaica. Anyway, I wish myself "All the Best". I also tell myself "man proposes and god disposes".

Convey my warm regards to friends and relatives.

You may give a few of them to Raghu and ask him to send them to a couple of personnel managers.

Hope to see you all by then, the end of 2002.

After reading this letter, father was almost in tears. For the first time in life, he said, "I don't want any financial help from my son! I will be happy to just see him. A sudden change came over father and he no longer expected money from Babu. He kept telling us, "If God gives me an opportunity to see my son, I shall be ever grateful to Him!" Day after day, we had to listen to his ramblings about his desire to see Babu.

I had learnt it the hard way not to get cowed down by failures of life and have also learnt to accept them in my stride. For, I have a strong faith in God and believe that God does the best for us. If we open our hearts to Him in full faith and pray sincerely, He was sure to fulfill all our desires and mitigate our sufferings. The feeling that I had brought about the doom of Babu already kept tugging at my heart and after reading his letter, I was now all the more bent upon helping him out of this miserable situation.

One optimistic note which I found in Babu's letter was his mention about a job in Kingston which he was looking forward to. I decided to commence a special prayer seeking God's blessings for Babu. I was determined to get him the Kingston job through my prayers!

42

Better Time are Coming

I found an old visiting card of Babu which I reverentially placed in the puja cupboard. Everyday, I offered special prayers to God seeking His blessings for the fruition of my brother's job. This special puja continued for almost fifty days. Each day, I would wake up with a positive feeling that Babu would phone up with some good news regarding the Kingston job. Somehow, I believed that God was sure to help him get the job. For, only then, will he be able to save some money and buy his airtickets and return to India. But Babu never called up. Months passed by and there was no news from him. This filled me with tension. One day I decided to take the first move. With my hands trembling, I called Babu. My heart thumped as Babu came on the line. He had probably been asleep and to my question whether he got the Kingston job or not, he said rather groggily, "Yes Hem! With all your prayers, I was able to succeed and I got the job. Better times are coming in to our lives and our future is going to be bright for all of us. I shall write to you in detail very soon!" Tears of happiness suffused my eyes! How kind is God ? He had indeed answered my prayers! Whoever has said that God is not there, has not approached Him with full faith and love!

Babu is going to earn well and he is going be a rich man soon. He is going to come back to India. And at last, I am going to see my loving brother. I was so thrilled and filled with excitement. All my burdens of life would come to an end. I would very soon be a free bird. The thought filled me with immense joy and already my imagination of a bright future was soaring high in my mind.

However, the fact that Babu himself did not phone up to me and convey the news first pained me so much. Why was he not anxious to tell us about the success in his job. What was holding him back from conveying the good news to us ? Did he change his plans about coming to India during the fag end of the year 2002 ?

43

Vow of Non-interference

Babu's promised letter giving details about his new job never reached us. Probably, he was now too busy to write to us. However, I kept phoning up to him once in two months requesting him about his plans of returning home. Each time he would assure me that he would call me back shortly confirming the dates. I would anxiously keep waiting for the call and after two months, when nothing was brewing, I would make another attempt of contacting him and would receive the same reply. This dilly-dallying continued for almost an year and the year 2003 was approaching its fag end.

My doubts about his home coming got intensified when my close friends and relatives started mocking at me. They said, "Hema, it is high time that you forget your brother and leave him alone. He is happily married and settled with a daughter. Now that he has got a well paid job, he would hardly think of returning back to India, leaving his family behind!"

However, this only further kindled the fire inside me. It was just for his homecoming that I spent hours in front of God praying that he should get the Kingston job. Now that he is financially secured, he is bound to visit his parents at least once. I was bent upon bringing him back to India and uniting him with the family, no matter what. Later, it was left to his discretion as to whether he wished to stay with us or return to Jamaica ; of which I had no say in the matter. But right now, I felt it was my responsibility to coerce him back to India. No one can change my mind over this. After-all, I have a strong faith in God and know pretty well that God would fulfil my wish. Until this goal is achieved, I will not have a peaceful sleep. I shall not become free of the guilt that is haunting me. This is a challenge which I consider very serious. And I did not wish to let anyone defy my challenge!

Once again, I decided to turn to God. One fine evening I stood in front of God and prayed at length :

"Oh God! You have been fulfilling all my wishes in life so far! Whatever I had prayed, you had fulfilled it for me. But when I pray that my brother should come down to India, you hardly seem to hear. I feel so guilty and pained at heart. In fact, I had been instrumental in praying to you and sending him to Jamaica. The purpose for which I had sent him did not meet with success. Instead, my family got ruined and is pushed to poverty. But right now, all I want is to see my brother. I don't want his money. Money is not at all important in life, I have realized. I vehemently long to see my brother and so are my parents. Oh God! I have made a blunder in sending him to Jamaica in the first place. Now I repent for my action and plead that you ought to send him back to us. I shall then never interefere in his life again. Since I had sent him to Jamaica, is it not my responsibility to bring him back ? I must at any cost bring about a union between my parents and their son. If any thing untoward happens in between, I shall never die in peace. Just once, Oh God, let me see my brother! Free me from the guilty feeling that had been plugging me for the past nine years.

I promise not to request him for any money. I just love to see him. I am dying to see him. Please God, Please, Please. . . . . !"

I finished my prayer shedding copious tears in front of Him and sobbed for quiet some time with my shoulders rocking. I had a feeling that God had listened to my prayers. I left the place with assurance.

44

You Win

My premonition was indeed right! For very soon, in December 2003, Babu called up one night. As soon as he heard my voice, he burst out cheerfully, "Hem, you win! I had at last decided to come down to India in April 2004. I shall be landing at 1.15 a. m. on 27th April 2004. I plan to be staying with you for a couple of months and then return to Jamaica!" My heart was throbbing inside my chest as I heard the good news from Babu and I said excitedly, "please keep up your word at least this time!" "Yes Hema. I am coming down for sure! But please tell all my folks not to expect any monetary help from me. I would not bring a single paise with me. I would be coming only with my clothes on!" With happiness writ large over my face, I retorted, "we don't need your money. We just want to see you and so please don't change your mind under any pretext!"

Happily, I conveyed the news to everyone. All of them were delighted to hear the good news and we were all looking forward to his arrival. Father started making a list of things he had to purchase before Babu's landing in India. Freshly ground coffee powder appeared first in his list. I wished to show off my house to Babu. Though it was six years old, I still considered it grand and moreover Babu was seeing it for the first time. A broken glass window in the dining hall was an eyesore and I requested my husband to get the same changed. Also, I told him to repair the minor crack in the bathroom wall. I wanted to present my house to him in all its grandeur. Further, I entertained my children with stories of my brother and they became very curious to see their uncle.

Raghu desired that the whole family should go to the airport to receive him. On 26th night I rang up to Babu to confirm his coming and his wife Maureen picked up the phone and informed me that he had already left for India. Mother could not accompany us and so Ramesh had to stay back with her. The rest of us with our children left the house at 11. 30 p. m in a van to the International airport at Meenambakkam. We were well ahead of the arrival time. There was an air of jubilation around us. We were waiting in the lounge with joy writ large on our faces to receive Babu after a period of nine long years and the children were merrily skating on the marble floor, running around each other. Father kept pacing across from one end to another looking around anxiously.

It was one of the happiest moments in my life! As I waited with abated breath for Babu, I kept thanking God for all His help. Finally, He had emancipated me from the mental turmoil I had been facing. I was at last free from the guilt that had been plugging my heart for nine long years. God had shown His presence to me by fulfilling my prayer and I was so thrilled. I was at peace with the world and felt like a free bird now. At the same time, I kept telling myself that I should henceforth show my love to God without any expectations from Him. He has done enough for me. He had fulfilled all the wishes of mine one after another. I decided not to request Him for fulfillment of any other favour in the future. Henceforth, I would never interfere in anybody's life – especially Babu's life! This time, I was determined to keep up my vow of non-interference, more than ever!

45

A Celebration Under the Moonlight

It was 1.15 a.m., when the arrival of the flight was announced. We gathered at the exit passage way to receive Babu. When at last Babu came into view, we all pointed our fingers towards him and shouted concomitantly, "there comes Babu!" With a smile on his face, he came towards us. He had bloated and had a French beard. All our eyes were on him.

Raghu introduced the new entrants into the family and he was able to recognize them easily and said, "I have seen your photos!" And at last, when his eyes met mine, words failed me. Tears imbued my eyes and I mustered up my strength and said, "It is like a dream come true, Babu!" And he smiled.

While returning home in the van, all of us kept staring at him. His way of speaking and mannerisms were quite different now. His accent was too difficult for me to understand. I had to ask him to repeat whatever he was saying so as to comprehend the same. All of a sudden, he looked at Raghu and gestured to him with his hand whether he would drink. I saw Raghu smiling slyly and nodding at him. A few minutes later, Babu said, "why don't we halt somewhere for a few seconds so that we can all have some juice!" Father interrupted him and said, "let's go home straight and no one is thirsty now!"

On reaching home, we saw mother sitting out in the veranda. It was 2. 30 a. m and she was waiting to see her son after nine long years. As soon as he entered, Babu hugged mother. Mother then took the *arathi* plate and circled camphor in front of him to ward off the evils. Babu was finding it rather difficult to converse with mother in Tamil. He told her that he had completely forgotten Tamil and mother assured him that he would recollect the language during his stay with her.

The whole family was sitting in the portico and celebrating Babu's reunion under the moonlight. After chatting with us for a while, my husband wished to make a move leaving me and my children to enjoy with my brother.

Babu showed us the photos of his wife and daughter. "You know Hem", he said. "It was my wife Maureen who forced me to start to India and see my parents. But for her, I would not be here! And you know, my daughter Krishna, she never let me go. She got into the big suitcase and shut herself in, asking me to carry her along with me!"

When I told Babu that I had taken a week's leave to be with him, his face brightened. "It is good that you have taken leave ; otherwise I would feel really bored!" he said.

He then entered the house and started examining the things one after another. He observed the old fridge which was now in shambles. "Is this the gas stove that I purchased before leaving,?" he asked me and I said yes. He then looked at the worn out condition of the walls and mused, "Pity! I really pity you all! I feel sorry for the poor condition of the house!" He then continued, "Hem, tomorrow, the first thing I wish to do is paint up the whole house. It is in a very bad plight!" I nodded my head silently.

I could see that Babu was extremely tired and suffered from jet lag. It was already 3. 00 a. m. I advised him to have some sleep and left the place after wishing him good night.

As I lay on the floor, I pinched myself several times to confirm if the whole thing happening around me was real or just a dream. It was a victorious moment in my life. The culmination of all my hard efforts to bring Babu back home at last met with success and I felt like a great winner. Babu was back among us once again! After nine long years! It was one of the happiest moments in my life. I was a free bird now. Thanking God for making the impossible happen ; for freeing me from the guilt that had been tormenting me all these years, I closed my eyes and slowly drifted away to a peaceful sleep.

46

The Painter at Work

Early in the morning, as I got up from bed, I saw Babu frantically searching for something. He was holding a roll of toilet paper in his hand and requested father for a match box. While handing him one, father wished to know the reason for the same. Babu then explained to him that he wanted to light his cigarette. He further confessed to father that without a cigarette in his hand, he would not be able to go to the toilet. Though it seemed very absurd to father, he left the place silently without offering any comment.

Later, Babu commenced painting the walls earnestly. While doing his job in great perfection, he stopped his work from time to time and apprised us with stories of Jamaica. He spoke a lot about his wife Maureen and daughter Krishna. "You know Hem", he began as usual. "To my wife this painting job is a child's play. She used to be of great assistance to me in running my workshop. She is a hard worker and nothing is impossible for her!"

It was around 9 a. m when father brought him a cup of hot coffee but Babu refused to have it and told him that he had stopped drinking coffee and tea. Though I informed him that father had purchased the special brand of freshly ground coffee powder just for his sake, Babu declined to drink it.

After sometime, he stopped his painting job and went up to meet Raghu. When he did not return for a long time, I was curious to find out what was holding him there. I ran up at once and what I saw shocked me. Babu was sitting with a glass of wine in his hand and Raghu was giving company to him. I became speechless and without uttering a word got down.

When at last Babu came down to continue his painting job, he said, "due to tension and hard work, I have become a prey to smoking and drinks. However, I love and respect my parents a lot. I promise I will never do this inside the house or in front of them!" Babu could not however continue with the painting job beyond a day. Father had to hire two men to get the whole house painted.

Frequently Babu would disappear from the house. He would either be standing alone in the rear side of the house puffing a cigarette or would be sitting with Raghu with a glass in his hand drinking. Soon, he would dissolve into a fit of giggles and proceed to launch into a cheerful rendition of some interesting stories about his life in Jamaica.

I found a sudden change in Raghu. He had become too condescending to his elder brother and carried out all errands for him in a jiffy. He immediately provided some space in his cupboard for Babu to store his drinks and cigarettes and gave him company during his drinks and listened patiently to whatever he had to say.

However, I disapproved of Babu indulging in this kind of pleasure. Though I had an aversion to see him with his glass of drink, I never voiced my opinion to him. I was very careful to keep my mouth shut, lest I deviate from the vow of non-interference that I had taken in front of God that resulted in the fruition of my prayer of bringing Babu back home.

Two days later, we were all assembled together for a chat in Raghu's house and Babu was in a very exulted mood. "Hem, it is so nice that all of us are here together. It is a happy moment indeed. I don't know how it is going to be tomorrow ; but today, I wish to thank God for this great moment". He then opened his large suitcase and took out a few dresses which he brought for all of us. He distributed a few shirts to each one of us. While handing over a dark green T –Shirt and a checked grey shirt with the words Sean John printed on it, he said, "Hem, promise me that you won't be giving this away to anybody. It is a very costly shirt and if you wear this in Jamaica, people will keep staring at you. It is the one worn by the affluent kind of people only!" I had been wishing to present my husband with a green T-shirt for a long while and the fact that I received one from Babu thrilled me to a great extent.

After distributing the clothes, he went in and helped himself to a glass of drink. Seeing him, my stomach started to churn. I tried to control my emotions and remained taciturn and decided not to question him about his frequent drinks. However, at this point of time, my sister Usha voiced her concern regarding his bad habit. "You seem to have become an addict to drinks. Why don't you put a full stop to this habit after taking some treatment. If you don't pay any attention to my advice, you are sure to ruin your health!"

But Babu was in no mood to listen to her. Instead, he started justifying his act in a very gleeful manner, "you see, I am just having a small cup of RUM. You know what RUM means. RUM stands for "Recommended Universal Medicine". It is in fact a health tonic. Eversince I have been having this, I have never felt the need to visit a doctor. It makes me feel energetic after all the hard work I do during the day. For your kind information, even before coming to India, I had gone for a general medical checkup and everything is normal! In Jamaica, people keep working hard till 2. 00 p. m. Later in the evening, they start drinking and dancing and enjoy life to the fullest!" Then, he went up to Usha and said, "just have a sip ; it tastes so good you know!" He had probably entered into a rum induced jovial mood and Usha immediately shoved him off.

47

Beginning of a Story

It was the fourth day after Babu's arrival at home. I was still bubbling with excitement over his return. That afternoon, my daughter attended puberty. This infact elevated my joy further. My little daughter has now become a young woman. I was now in a fix whether to let the news out or keep it a secret. Father was of the opinion that I keep taciturn regarding this for a while. But mother insisted that a small function be held inviting close relatives. While I was in a dilemma as to whose side I should take, Babu butted in, "Hem, she is your daughter and you and your husband have to take a decision regarding this and not your parents." I later decided to have a small function as suggested by mother. One evening, Babu told me, "you know Hem, once my daughter comes of age, I would leave Jamaica and return to India. It is only now that she seeks my company. Later on, she would find a boy friend when I would be no more required for her. In Jamaica, girls as young as 12 years old can be seen roaming with a boy friend. So it will be another four years stay in Jamaica and then I will return home. Wondering at his cool manner over his daughter's life and the casual lifestyle of the people of Jamaica, I said, "you must tell me all about yourself and about the life you led in Jamaica in great detail. Someday, I plan to write a book about you! May be we can sit together for sometime tomorrow because my leave will be over in a few days and it will be time to join office." I also invited him to my house and he agreed to come along with me.

The next afternoon, when I saw Babu relaxing in a chair, I went and sat in front of him and requested him to begin his story. I found that Babu was restless and he was looking around for something. Suddenly, he stood up and excused himself for a shortwhile. Then in a few minutes he returned with a glass of wine and sat down happily. Raghu who passed by was quick to reprimand him, "how dare you drink in front of Hema ? You know she is against drinks!" But Babu responded in a cool manner, "Hema has changed now! She has become more mature in life and she would pardon me for the same. " Though I felt offended to see him with his wine glass, I knew that he needed it to talk to me and so I reluctantly nodded my head without looking at his face. He then began his story.......

After I said goodbye to all of you at the airport and left the place, my eyes welled up. I walked ahead without turning back. When my flight reached Mumbai airport, I had to face much hardship at the British Embassy. I was not permitted to board my connecting flight to London. They interrogated me for a long time. They asked me, why should I, a young man of Twenty Three years only chose to go to Jamaica of all places on earth for a job. They advised me that, many opportunities are available in Gulf countries for my profession and asked me several times if I was sure about the decision I had taken to leave India for Jamaica.I then explained to them that, after two months, my working place will be shifted to United States and that is why I had accepted this offer. This answer convinced them, and I was let to board my connecting flight to London.

On reaching London too, I was thoroughly checked. Probably, they suspected me to be carrying drugs or something. For later, I heard funny stories of how people duped the personnel at the security check counter by hiding drugs in their bodies. Some even go to the extent of cutting their breasts in order to place the drugs inside them. After I was through with the verification, I left London airport and got into a bus that was waiting outside and settled comfortably. The bus went round and round and finally returned to London Airport. I got down much embarrassed and decided to seek help. I had to come out of my shell. I understood that inhibition and shyness will get me nowhere.

At first, the accent of Londoners was confusing to me. Then I listened to them carefully and also requested them to repeat the sentence again and again till I understood what they said. Slowly, I got used to their accent. One kind airport official understood my predicament. He explained to me that I now needed to board another connecting flight to the Heathrow Airport which stopped at Jamaica. Further, he held my hand and whisked me along to the flight and I got into it just a few minutes before its take off. I realized that I was so stupid not to have clarified my doubts before.

48

Babu Becomes Sam

When I reached Jamaica Airport, I looked around anxiously for some assistance.I was filled with joy to see a middle aged man standing there with a placard marked "Sampath Kumar". The man had a beard and but for this, he was exactly like our father in his young days. I went up to him and introduced myself. Within a few minutes of talking to him, I gathered some information about him. He was a Christian and a kind hearted man. He did not smoke or drink and was a teetotaler. He then asked me, "now tell me, how do I address you ? Shall I call you Sam, Sampath or Kumar ?" And I readily told him that he could call me as he wished. He chose Sam because that was easy for him. Slowly, everyone started to call me Sam. In Jamaica, wherever I go, people recognize me as Sam – the man who repairs airconditioners and fridges.

I told him that I did not relish the food that was offered to me in the flight.Further, I explained to him that since I had not eaten properly, I was really famished and requested him to get me some vegetarian food. In fact, I was looking forward to some sambhar, rasam and curd rice. But the man regretted and informed me that such foods would not be available in the hotels and that almost all hotels in Jamaica serve only non-vegetarian food. I was shocked to hear this. I told him that I was a pure vegetarian and would not like to enter these non-vegetarian hotels. Seeing my pleading look on my face, he decided to help me out. He informed me that just a few weeks back, another Indian had joined the company. He had come along with his family and he at-once took me to their house. He requested the lady to prepare some vegetarian food specially for me and she obliged. I had my fill and thanked them profusely for their kind gesture.

Later on, I was taken to my lodge, which was situated on top of a hill. It was surrounded by trees all around. The greenery was a feast to one's eyes. A short walk from my lodge leads to a beach. Also, one could see plenty of waterfalls and beaches all along the way in Jamaica. You can also see lush orange trees on both sides of the roads as you pass by. Often I would see people stop by to pluck oranges.They would squash them with their hands and drink up the juice to quench their thirst.

The next day, I went to meet Mr. Narayanan. After the formal introductions were over, Narayanan took me to his farm. It was a large farm of about 18 acres.The farm was a beautiful bed of pretty and colourful flowers. The workers in the farm scared me out of my wits. They were looking like the gypsies and each one had a long knife or a gun to safeguard themselves.They spoke a language called Pattois which is nothing but broken English. They have long hair and if you stare at them, they would get scared and provoked and would go to the extent of even killing you. I was first scared of speaking to these people but slowly I tried to make friends with them and realized they were harmless.

Narayanan then started to explain my nature of job. He said that he cultivated flowers to make boquets and sell them to countries like Miami, New York and United States. The workers here gather the flowers and make fresh bouquets out of these. My job was to count these bouquets and carry them in an airconditioned truck to the Santacruz Airport from where it would be shipped to different countries. The most difficult job was to drive on the hilly roads as they were too curved and by mistake if you lose your grip on the wheel, you would get thrown off the road and that's the end of your life. And one who knows to drive in these hilly roads is surely an ace international driver.

I was in fact shocked to learn about the job that I was delegated.I explained to Narayanan that I was an AC and Refrigeration Engineer and that counting bouquets and transporting them had nothing to do with my profession. Further, I curtly told him that I did not like the job that he was assigning me and requested him to consider me for some other engineering job. This set about a misunderstanding between us and led to a big fight of which you are already aware of through my letters. Narayanan was a stubborn and stone hearted fellow and he did not oblige me. Having no other alternative, I continued to work in his farm. In the meanwhile, I had also started looking for a better job elsewhere.

49

Job at the Rum Factory

I slowly got accustomed to the lifestyle in Jamaica. At first, I detested to even enter a non vegetarian hotel. But at the same time, I did not wish to trouble my other Indian counterparts who had come there with their family. Hence, there being no way out, I slowly started to enter the non vegetarian hotels and requested the hotel owners to prepare some vegetarian food specially for me. Though they agreed to do so, all they could provide me was plain rice with vegetable curry mostly peas as that was available in plenty in Jamaica. In fact, Jamaicans love these peas and this is one secret of their robust health. To me, it was a great wonder to see seventy year old men and women playing with young children running about happily and with much vigour. Fed up of a typical diet, slowly I started tasting some other varieties of dishes made from eggs, fishes and chickens as well. I became a non-vegetarian.

Except for the food problem that I encountered there, Jamaica is otherwise a place of natural beauty and pleasure. It is the place where one can enjoy life to the utmost. For, it is a free country where there is no law. People indulge in smoking, drinking and sex in a very carefree manner. Like you have tea stalls at every nook and corner, in Jamaica every street has a bar. Drinks are available in plenty and they are also so cheap. In fact, some of the world famous drinks are manufactured here in Jamaica. Some of the bars are nude bars. As you enjoy your drink, you can watch a nude dance and if you so desire, you can even pick up a girl and go out. I was however never interested in these affairs.

I got along with Narayanan for almost six months. Eventually, I realized that he was in no way going to change my job portfolio and decided to make a move from there. The fact that I had to fend for myself filled me with fear. Penniless and on the streets, I approached our Indian Embassy and explained my predicament to them. The man who heard my story patiently offered to help me out of the situation and requested me to come the next day. With great anticipation I went to see him the next day. I was rather shocked to note that the very same person who had been kind to me the previous day was rather rude to me. His condescending tone was gone and he advised me that since it was all my doing, I had to try and come out of the situation myself. Further, he said that his hands were tied and he could do nothing to relieve me from the imprisoned life that I presently landed myself in. I bet that it was all the handiwork of that merciless guy Narayanan. Probably, he must have bribed him or something. God will never forgive that fellow.

No wonder, the guy has no kids! One of my friends found me a job in a rum factory. Different kinds of drinks were being manufactured here. My job was to take care of the AC Plant there. Also, tourists from all over the world came to have a look at this rum factory. I had also to take them around and explain the manufacturing process to them, giving them a sample of each of the drinks that we had formulated. Before doing this chore, I had to first of all have a sip of these drinks to test their quality, prior to offering it to the visitors. That is how I slowly got into the habit of drinking.

I had by now made a few Jamaican friends who were rather very kind to me. The expiry date of my passport and visa was fast approaching. I was filled with tension. I had to decide between the two options that were available to me. One was that I had to pack up and leave Jamaica immediately. I could not go ahead with this because I did not have sufficient funds to buy my air tickets. The other option as advised by my friends was to get married to a Jamaican girl which would enable me to get the citizenship of the country. This also gave me an opportunity to continue my stay till I desired to.

While I was in a fix and anxious about my next step that I had to take, my friends coaxed me to first get married to a Jamaican girl and also volunteered to find me one. They told me that it was just a makeshift arrangement to just prolong my stay in Jamaica until I earned my airtickets. Or if I so wished, I could also look out for a better job with a good salary and be of help to my family. I had no other alternative and was forced to abide by their suggestion. My friends set about with the task of finding a suitable match for me. The fact that I was looking around for a girl to be my temporary wife spread across the Parish quickly. One girl whom my friends introduced demanded a fee of 50,000 J$ for this job and I curtly refused to accept her.

In the meanwhile, I had vacated the lodge that Narayanan had given me and was now hunting around for a small house with a low rent that I could afford. A word of this also got around. Very soon my friends gave me the address of a landlady who was willing to rent her house and one evening I went to meet her.

50

The Kind of Land Lady

I shall never forget this evening in my life. Though I was satisfied with the house that the landlady showed to me, I could not afford to pay the huge rent of 1500 J$. So, rejecting her offer, I slowly kept walking back in a very depressed mood, when all of a sudden, a woman in her thirties stopped me. She asked, “Sir, are you looking around for a house in this area?” When I answered her in the affirmative, she said that she had a small room which she was willing to rent and requested me to accompany her. I inspected the small house and was satisfied with it. When she told me that the rent was just 450 J$ per month, I readily agreed to move in. Though it was a very compact house, I was much impressed with it. The lady then introduced herself as Maureen.

The following week, I had brought in my belongings and settled in my new abode. Maureen had a young and cute girl whose name was Nadia. Slowly, Nadia got much attached to me and quite often, she would barge into my room and enjoy playing or listening to my stories. Day after day, Nadia started to spend more time with me and I adored her a lot. I would entertain her with jokes and stories which she cherished and also helped her in her studies. Maureen would often come looking for her in my room and she would not leave without having a small conversation with me.

Slowly, Maureen started to be of help to me in several ways. I would generally soak my clothes in a bucket after bathing and leave for work intending to wash them in the evening. On my return from work, I would be astonished to see them all neatly washed and fastened to the clothesline. On some days, when I returned home very late, Maureen would enter my room carrying a plate of hot rice, peas and some dry fish and request me to eat. Though I was taken away by her kindness, I wondered why she was doing all this for me.

51

The Temporary Wife

During work in the rum factory one day, I had an argument with my friend. I challenged him that though I had tasted all types of drinks that his country had to offer, nothing was really strong enough to intoxicate me and lift up my spirits. My Jamaican friend had taken this statement rather too seriously and he immediately offered a special drink to me. It was a rum which appeared to be white in colour. It was indeed a strong rum that did strange things to my body. Rather it affected my body so badly that I had to rush home and could not continue my work. As soon as I reached home, I started vomiting and also felt giddy. When Maureen saw me vomiting continuously, she volunteered to help me out. She gave me some pills and requested me to sleep. But when I started to close my eyes, I felt the urge to vomit again. Seeing me struggle out of bed, Maureen came running and cupped both her hands in front of me and asked me to vomit into it. This kind gesture on her part shocked me beyond belief. Further, she wiped my mouth with water and left the place. Within half-an-hour she returned once again with a plate of hot food and started feeding me. She gave me more pills to swallow and I immediately fell asleep. It was around 4 a.m. early in the morning when I woke up. I could not believe my eyes when I saw that the lights were still on and Maureen was sitting near my bed fighting her drowsiness. After verifying with me if I was feeling better, she took leave of me.

That day, I could not concentrate much on my work. I kept pondering over the strange behaviour of Maureen ; wondering all the while as to why she was fussing over me so much ? Why was she exhibiting such affection towards me ? Was she in love with me ? Doubts began to assail my mind. However, I reserved my doubts to myself. But very soon, Maureen herself broke the ice. One fine evening, she came to me and said, "I understand that you are planning to extend your stay in Jamaica and that you are looking for a girl to be your wife for a short period!" When I nodded my head, she continued, "if you don't mind, I would like to be your temporary wife!" I was startled by her boldness and became speechless. However, gathering up my courage, I said, "you have a daughter and you must be already married to someone!" She then told me that her parents were staying in United States and she had two brothers as well. She had come to Jamaica to study and was staying with her grandmother. While studying in college, she chanced to meet a Chinese man who fell in love with her. During the short stint of their love affair, Nadia was born. It was actually an accident and Nadia was infact born out of wedlock. The fellow got involved in drugs and finally turned insane. And when the baby was six months, he left her and got settled in Canada and that she had nothing to do with him now.

Since it was a temporary arrangement, I gave my concurrence to her. I firmly told her that I was getting married to her just to prolong my stay for a while and once I earned my air-tickets, I would leave for India.

52

An Angel

The marriage took place in a church. It was a very simple one. Maureen had invited two of her best friends and so did I. Slowly Maureen stopped collecting the rent from me and she also requested me to move in to her room along with my things. Her kind acts one after another made me fall in love with her. One day she broached the subject of sex and told me that she was taking birth pills every day. I understood her intentions and gradually entered in to sex life. This was a time when I rather got too mesmerized in life and forgot our family for a while. I left the job at the rum factory and Maureen helped me to open a bar to sell drinks. I was indeed making some money out of it.

Now, I decided to do some real business concerning my profession. Maureen once again helped me set up a small workshop to repair fridges, airconditioners and other home appliances. She also joined me in servicing the gadgets. Together we made quite a lot of money. But when I got a better offer in a reputed company, a few kilometers away from my house, I abandoned my workshop and joined the company.

One evening Maureen rang me up and said, "Sam, I have some bad news for you!" While I was wondering what the bombshell was going to be, she continued, “Sam, today I had gone to see the doctor for a checkup. I was in fact worried about my stomach which started bulging all of a sudden. The doctor informed me that I was pregnant by eight months and I just can't believe it. He also told me that it was too late for an abortion as well. I wonder how this has happened despite my taking the birth pills regularly apart from having regular periods! I also did not experience any kind of morning sickness or any other symptoms that pregnant women generally faced!” My heart leapt into my throat on hearing the news and it took considerable time for me to digest the fact. However, that night I told her that we could have the baby since God had forced her into our hands and also it was too late for an abortion. When the baby was finally born, I decided to give her an Indian name and hence we called her Krishna Kumar. She came into our lives unexpectedly and I consider her as God's gift to me. She is the angel of my life.

53

Disagreement Over Biknis

As Krishna started growing, she got too attached to me. When I returned home from work, she would excitedly come crawling towards me calling, "dada, dadá" and my heart would melt immediately. I got too attached to my new family that God had set up in my life. Due to this bondage in Jamaica, I was transported into a different world altogether and I was slowly drifting away from you people. I also stopped talking and writing to you and to be frank the thought of returning to India was etched out from my mind. I had become a Jamaican in toto.

I adopted Nadia and she became my step daughter. On one hand Krishna was stealing my heart and on the other, I also felt that it was my duty to be financially supportive to Maureen and Nadia. I spent a lot of money in educating Nadia. Of course, I did this with a selfish motive. I believed that if anything untoward happened to me or I had to leave the country on an emergency, I wanted Nadia to step into my shoes and take care of my loving daughter and Maureen. I always wished that my daughter should lead a very rich and secured life.

However, our marital life was not bereft of quarrels. Maureen and I would often disagree over Nadia. I had always wanted to bring her up the Indian way. But Nadia disliked this. She wanted to wear biknis and tight fittings exposing her body. She also wished to spend the weekends with her friends and when I insisted that I too would accompany her, she would not let me do this. There were always a group of boys following her and some of them would also be lingering around the house. Maureen would have a tough time hurling stones at them to drive them out from there. Time and again I would advice Nadia that since she was already beautiful, there was no necessity for her to expose her body or flaunt around with sexy dresses in order to attract boys. She would never understand. She wanted freedom like the other Jamaican girls.

The women in Jamaica have more than three or four husbands. Maureen's grandmother has twenty seven children out of nine husbands. Unlike in India, the children get scattered around and fend for themselves and do not stay with their parents for long. With this background, Maureen herself was supportive of her and held the same views as Nadia and this always resulted in a misunderstanding between us. Finally I realized my folly and gave up my attempts to transform Nadia into an Indian girl..... .

It was already turning into dusk and I could see that Babu was feeling rather tired. Finally, as he stood up, he said, "well, I have summed up my nine years story in a nutshell. I will tell you about the culture, custom and lifestyle of the Jamaicans tomorrow. "

54

Health is Wealth

That night, sleep evaded me for a long time. I kept ruminating over the story I had heard from Babu. I was very disappointed over the enormous changes that the country had brought upon him. It had made him an addict to drinks, which in turn had affected his health as well. He often complained of headaches and pain in his hands and legs. This was a real shock to me.

I was disheartened by his addiction to drinks. However, I stuck to my vow of non-interference and kept silent over this. In fact, I was tongue-tied due to the promise I made to God. But when others reproached him for this, I felt quite happy.

Babu was either smoking or drinking all the time. Once when mother pointed this out to him and begged him to stop this habit and also shed copious tears, he became wild. "Ma, I did not come here to see you cry", he shouted at her. "If you cry again, I shall pack up and leave for Jamaica", he threatened her. After this, mother stopped advicing him for she did not wish to miss her son. However, father was clever enough and he kept harping upon this fact indirectly by telling him, "Babu, health is wealth! Don't forget this and try to take care of your health first!" But this advice too fell on his deaf ears but however he would never retort to father.

He had brought 3000 J$ along with him and got the same converted into Indian cash. He gave this to father and asked him to enjoy himself. But ultimately, he requested father to return the money and used it to buy cigarettes and drinks. After spending this, he turned to me and sought financial help. And every time, he took the cash from my hand, he would say, "Hem, I promise to return every single pie I borrow from you, once I reach Jamaica!"

He had not given up his anger even now. He continued to remain a short-tempered fellow and got offended quickly. He was a morose person and always sat brooding about something or the other. But once he had his drinks, he would become a very jovial person and start talking affectionately to everyone. He would crack jokes and make every one laugh. He would also start playing games with the kids. At times, he would proceed to launch into a cheerful rendition of some interesting stories about his life in Jamaica. In a charming manner, he would keep us all enthralled for a long time.

On some days, he would go up to meet Raghu early in the morning. He would never return till evening. He would sit drinking and sharing his emotions and problems with Raghu. Sometimes, he would become too excited and request Raghu to switch on the tape recorder. He would then start swinging round in an exaggerated dance routine and entertain everyone with variety of Jamaican dances.

55

The Missing Month in the Calender

On the next day, when I sat with Babu for having a chat, he started complaining about how he was missing his daughter terribly.........

Hem, I miss my daughter a lot! She is my angel and heart beat. It is just for her that I am planning to return to Jamaica. Yesterday night when I spoke to her, Maureen told me that her vacation had just begun and she is missing her daddy a lot. Learning that I would return only in the month of August, she tore off the May, June and July sheets from the calendar. For she wished to see only the month of August when her daddy would come back to her. My wife complained to me that very often, she would lie down on the bed and start screaming for daddy and that she is having a tough time controlling her tantrums.

Well, let me continue with my story. In Jamaica, the climate is a tropical one. The mornings are very hot and at about 2.00 p.m. it starts to rain. The source of water is rain. Every house has a small tank to collect the rain water and store it for future use.The rain here is often accompanied by hail stones. This often destroys the tomatoes and peas which are cultivated in plenty.

People eat natural foods processed from peas and wheat. They make a smooth dough of wheat flour and make thick and flat chappatis which look like buns. They immerse it in salt water and boil it. Later on, they eat them with non-vegetarian side dishes. Each person would eat six to seven pieces of this kind. That is why their life span is very high. You can see people as old as 80 or 90 years old playing with their kids energetically. Jamaicans do their work by themselves. They don't have servant maids at home. They work hard in the fields upto 2. 00 p. m and in the evening, they enjoy drinking and dancing.

The mode of transport in the cities is only cars. Car pooling is very common in Kingston. Four to five persons who work in the same place join together and use one car. This way, they avoid the peak hour traffic jam. For the people in the country, the mode of transport is usually horse or donkeys.

In Jamaica, dressing is very obscene. Girls wear bikinis and t-shirts or simply bras. They do this to attract men. A small scramble attached to the television will enable you to watch blue films continuously. That is why the theatres are empty most of the time. People have great belief in hoodooism. It is a special prayer offered to God to bring about the downfall of an enemy. The enemy undergoes both mental and physical pain due to this. And the Jamaicans have a great faith in this kind of hoodooism. People also believe in the so called spiritual oils. They have different varieties of oil for different purposes. Some of these bring either luck, money, success in love, marriage or business. People are crazy about these oils and they apply these on their bodies to get their wishes fulfilled. The Jamaicans are indeed very kind to Indians and the foreigners who visit their country and they treat them with love and respect. They celebrate New Year and Christmas with great pomp and show. The Indians living there join together and celebrate Diwalli at the Indian embassy.

56

The Nude Island

Finally, I should tell you something about the nude island. You know Hem, once I had asked you for financial help and you had told me that you were helpless. However, you had offered prayers for me and I was lucky to get that Kingston job. I became a rich man after that. It was one of the best jobs in the world. It was a job in an all-inclusive hotel called Ocho Rio's Hotel. I was given a salary of 50000 J$ per month. I had plenty of money on hand. People started referring to me as the money man for whenever anyone was in need of financial help, I would give them money and not take it back. I had also spoilt my daughter a lot. I would take her to the supermarket and let her choose whatever she wanted.

I was appointed as Chief Engineer and around thirty men were under my control. The hotel was situated in about 19 acres of land. There was a ground attached to this hotel for polo and I learnt horse riding here. I was given a posh bungalow with three bedrooms and a swimming pool. A Security Guard was also posted here for my security. I lived alone in this bungalow and it was during the weekends that my wife and daughter would join me. My daughter would get so enchanted and she would go around from one room to another in her tricycle enjoying herself.

There is a beach near this hotel. This beach is famous for its nude island which is also attached to this hotel. This nude island is situated in the middle of the beach and one has to take a boat to reach this nude island. The practice here is that the people should take off their clothes and remain nude. It is a very small island with many bars and caffes attached to it. People from all over the world lavish their money in lakhs to reach this nude island and enjoy themselves by drinking and smoking. Many a time, I was asked to go to this nude island to attend to some maintenance problems. Ofcourse, I was allowed to go in with my dress. During such times, I would see many Indians too. Some of them would be too shy to remove their dresses and so stay back in the boat itself. They would however see the nude island through the binoculars.

It was while I was working in Ocho Rio's hotel, that I started drinking on a daily basis. As long as I had a Jamaican boss, I had no problem. I could get along with them smoothly. They would advice me in a friendly manner to stop drinking. It was only when I was asked to report to an Indian boss that problems started cropping up. We could not get along. He would tell me not to drink while coming to the workplace.A fight would ensue due to this. All my workers used to tell me that I was a terrific guy in the mornings and they would not approach me for anything. They would tell me that I had two different personalities. For in the evenings, I would go to the bar and they would join me there and we would all have a drink together and enjoy ourselves.

I could not get along with him for we were having frequent quarrels and he was making my life miserable. I had to resign my job. It was one of the best jobs in the world that I gave up due to my temper. Somehow, I was not able to get along anywhere because of my bad temper which I could not give up. However, by this time, I had saved enough money and Maureen requested me to visit India and see my parents. You were also constantly phoning up to me and calling me and so I am here. I used up all my savings to buy my airtickets and now I have become penniless. If I go back to Jamaica, I will have to start my life all over again. I don't have a single pie with me.

57

A Question Out of the Blue

Babu was getting restless all of a sudden. He stood up and excused himself for a while. He went to smoke, leaving me alone; pondering over his life. When was he going to settle in life ? Would he ever settle in his life ? Will he be of any help to father in settling his loans ? For all this to happen, first of all, he had to stop losing his temper. His anger was hampering his progress in life. Despite being aware of this, he was not showing any signs of improving his character. In fact, his anger was getting from bad to worse. He was not willing to correct himself nor listen to anybody's counseling.

Though I was disappointed over Babu's life, I was firm and did not wish to interfere in his life or offer any advice to him. The fact that Babu was now physically present with us was a matter of great joy to me. And this was possible only after I had taken a vow of non-intereference in his life once God granted my wish of uniting Babu with the family. And now I wished to be thankful to Him by fulfilling my promise.

Before going to sleep that night, I noticed that Babu was agitated and tensed over something. However, paying no attention to this, I wished him goodnight and went to bed. He kept walking restlessly from one end of the room to the other silently. It was midnight, when all of a sudden, I woke up with a start. The lights were still on and I saw Babu standing near the window peering outside. When I asked him why he had not gone to sleep yet, he said, "Hem, I miss my family and I am just thinking of my daughter!" Slowly, he walked towards my bed and sat down beside me. Then he continued, "Hem, I am going to ask you a question and I want a honest reply from you!" While I sat benumbed wondering what he was going to ask me at this hour, he continued in a very depressing tone, "Hem, tell me if I have committed a sin in my life. Have I been unfair in life ? You may take your own time, but you must be truthful in your answer!"

His question was out of the blue at the odd hour and I became dumbfounded. I was myself not sure of the answer. I could have given vent to my anger by berating him for his unjust behaviour and ruining our family by being very careless. I could have bawled out at him for taking thoughtless decisions in his life. I could have screamed at him for not turning my dreams into reality and betraying all of us down here. However, I did none of these. Age and the experiences I had gained in life had transformed me into a person of serene personality which made me think in a very rational way.

I was suddenly filled with pity for him. I deliberated upon the question for a moment. Whatever be the case, I did not wish to hurt his feelings. In a very scrupulous manner, I responded, "Babu, you yourself know the answer to this! Your own concience is well aware of it! But then, you were helpless! You could do nothing about the circumstances that you were thrown into. This is what we call fate! It was your destiny which made you behave like that and made you do the things you did and so were we destined to suffer in poverty."

Probably, he was contented with my reply. For he did not get into his usual debating nor disputed with me over that. After a long silence, he said, “Hem, you have given me a very diplomatic answer! You have indeed become a matured person in life!” His words were so gratifying to my ears.

58

Words That Was Music to Ears

My short vacation was coming to an end. I invited Babu to my house and he readily agreed. The next evening, when my husband came to pick me and the children up, Babu too accompanied us. As soon as he stepped into the house ; which he was seeing for the first time, he exclaimed, "Wow! It is a grand house indeed!" He kept admiring the house all the while and as he passed on from one room to another he was full of praise for me, "Hem, it is a cosy and posh house that you have built. I am really proud to be having a rich sister!" His pleasing words were music to my ears. I had in fact been longing to hear these words from him. I had not waited in vain.

Unlike in the past, when Babu was ready to carp or cavil at me for the trivial things I said or did, he was a changed person now. He was full of appreciation for me. After having a sumptuous dinner, Babu sat with us and posed for photographs. My children then showed him the old albums and I bragged to him about our trips to the Andaman & Nicobar islands and the Kullu Manalli Hills and about how I had also taken father along with us in the flight for the first time in Jet Airlines.

I requested him to stay with us for the night but he refused by telling me that he had already told Raghu to pick him up at 11 p. m. The truth was, he could not sleep without his drinks and knew pretty well that I would not permit him to have it inside my house. However, he promised to return a few days later and expressed his desire to see the film "Passion of Christ", the CD's of which were not available in Jamaica. The theatres were running this film and it was not easy to get the tickets for this film. I promised to get the CD of this film very soon.

Within a week I was able to procure the CD and I phoned up to Babu. He was so thrilled and immediately rushed home to see it. I too sat down beside him and saw the whole movie. Quite frequently, he got into a fit of tears while watching the film. Probably he had got too much involved in the film and enjoyed it wholeheartedly. He thanked me profusely for this kind gesture.

In the evening, before taking leave, he shared his woes with me. He said that the meagre amount that he carried along with him from Jamaica was fully spent and he was without a penny on hand now. Further, he expressed his desire to prepone his air ticket and proceed to Jamaica, for he did not wish to be a burden to father or anybody else. Once he lands up there, he could find a new job. I listened to his grouches silently without offering my views on that. However, my husband quickly handed over some cash to him and also assured him that there was no necessity for him to prepone his tickets and that if he was in need of any monetary help, he could always ring him up for help. Babu's face started brimming with happiness on hearing this and turning towards me he blurted out, "Hem, I am keeping an account of every single pie that I borrow from you. Once I return to Jamaica, I am sure to find a job and I promise to repay the whole amount to you. I shall be sending you a cheque very soon!" I smiled and informed him that I did not expect the money back. For this, he replied in a rather aggressive manner, "no Hem, I will be sending the cheque in your name and it is upto you to spend it as you wish!"

I then told him that instead of struggling to look out for a new job in Jamaica, he could join the same old Ochio Rio's Hotel again. He agreed that it was a good idea and was willing to give it a try.

As soon as I stepped into my room after giving Babu a send-off, it struck me. I had in fact messed up with my vow of non-interference by suggesting Babu to try in the Ochio Rio's Hotel. I chided myself for this and took a firm decision not to offer any advice to him again and bungle up his life.

59

Going Overboard to Please

We were all so mesmerized by Babu's homecoming. I was fascinated by his style and mannerisms which had drastically changed. His foreign accent of speaking also captivated me so much that at times, I would simply gape at him as he spoke. With his interesting stories, he would keep us enthralled for a long time. We got attracted towards him like a magnet.

The children too became very fond of him and got attached to him. Very often they would pile on top of him in a giggling scrimmage. Once when mother told Raghu's two year old daughter that Babu uncle would be leaving for Jamaica very soon, she became wild. She ran up to him and screamed, "don't go!". Babu then lifted her into his arms and explained to her, "I must go! I have a little daughter like you. She is my angel and heart beat. I love her so much. She would be missing me a lot and I cannot stay back without seeing her". He then turned towards me and said, 'I shall be coming next year for Diwalli with my family and settle down here. We shall then enjoy ourselves!"

It was for this reason that we could not ask Babu to stay back here. He convinced us that he had to return to Jamaica, no matter what, for he was missing his daughter so much. Babu liked my son a lot. Once, he drew him closer and said, "Hem, I love to have a cute son like this. But it will not be now. I will be settling down with my family next year and then I shall surely try for a son!"

Since Babu was here, we organised many get togethers by way of celebrating the birthdays of our children. During such occasions, Babu would become very joyous and say, "Hem it is indeed a very happy moment for me to see the whole family assembled together. " He would mumble a prayer to God and then continue, "we must thank God for giving us this opportunity. We don't know how it is going to be tomorrow. But let us all enjoy ourselves to the utmost today!"

Suddenly he would disappear from the room. A few minutes later, I would be shocked to see him with a glass of drink in his hand, chatting enthusiastically and supervising the serving of dishes. Cigarettes and drinks brought great happiness to him. And the pretext he used for this was that he was missing his family so much and just to forget them he was having his drinks. Though he was on a binge, continuously drinking from dawn to dusk, he looked and behaved in a sober way. However, on seeing him with a glass of drink, my stomach would start to churn. Immediately, I would start worrying as to why he was ruining his health by drinking and making a fool of himself. But outwardly, I would smile at him and pretend that it was all good fun.

We siblings were vying with each other to please Babu. All his requests and demands were quickly met by us without any hesitation or delay. At times, we would go over-board and endeavour to please him in the best way we could. During the weekends when I went to see him, I would buy plenty of sweets and savories for him. After relishing the same, he would comment, "Hem, I am proud to be having a loving sister!"

My sister on the other hand would go a step further. She would exert herself by making some of his favourite snacks at home itself and take it to him. At times, on his humble pleas, she would go out of the way and indulge herself in doing the arduous task of buying cigarettes for him.

Raghu was readily available to him at his beck and call. He would patiently hear him out by giving company to him throughout the day. At length, Babu would talk to him about his future plans and the business venture he wished to start in the future.

Once when Raghu was away on a short trip for two days with his family, Babu was forced to spend his time with my youngest brother Ramesh. During this time, he taught him to ride the motorbike and also advised him to get married soon. And once when Babu coaxed him to buy a bottle of drink for him ; at first he disapproved of it. But finally, he found himself standing in front of a wine shop carrying out the errand for him.

I had an aversion to even look at the person smoking a cigarette or having a drink. But one fine day, when my husband came home with a big box of imported cigarettes and asked me to give it to Babu as gift, my face lit up with a smile. Though I was aware that I would be further damaging his health, the fact that I would get to see the excitement on his face as he received it from me, made me grab it from his hands. My husband who was quick to notice the smile remarked rather sarcastically, "you always enjoy doing things gratis for your family.

60

A Gift of the Black Leather Purse

Five months had elapsed since Babu's arrival. The month of September had at last arrived. The days had flown by so swiftly and now it was time for Babu to leave. Our spirits fell low at the thought of Babu's return to Jamaica.

Babu turned gloomy all of a sudden. From being a very cheerful person, he now changed into a depressed one and always looked sullen. Whenever he spoke to me, his eyes glistened with tears and in a dismal tone, he would say, "Hem, I am going to miss all of you! I just can't leave you people and go back to Jamaica! It is just for my daughter that I am going back!" I would have a tough time in consoling him. "Babu, you really don't have to worry so much. Afterall, you are planning to come down next year and the time will fly off quickly. The world is becoming a smaller place day after day. People are now talking of honeymooning and picnicking in space. With the internet and the cell phones we can always stay connected and meet very soon!" He would however never get convinced with my explanation and burst out with fresh tears.

Two days before his departure, he stopped eating rice and when mother coaxed him, he said, "Ma, I had been enjoying life with you people. But once again, I should start getting used to hardships. I am not going to get these delicious foods in Jamaica. It is time that I change over to a Jamaican once again!"

On the day of his departure, I was rummaging my cupboards for some things that I could give to Babu as presents to carry to his wife and daughter. My other siblings had already presented him with their share of gifts and Babu had neatly stacked them in his travel bag. Once when my son became curious and wished to see the contents of his bag, Babu disapproved of it by telling him, "even if you drop a small blade into it by mistake, I will not be able to pass the security check!" By evening, I had collected few nighties and earrings for Maureen and a few story books, frocks, chains, bangles and pens for Krishna. While I was on the job, Babu called up and requested me for two things. He wanted a small purse to keep all his cards and another was a ring studded with green stone. In fact, I did have one black expensive leather pouch, which I had been preserving for a long time and wished to give it away as a gift to someone I loved and valued a lot. When Babu asked for it, I immediately decided to present the same to him. I also succeeded in procuring a silver ring with a green stone at the centre.

On 13th of September 2004, around 9. 00 p. m, the whole family had gathered together to accompany Babu to the airport. Babu's eyes were red in colour. One reason was that he had been crying like a child at the thought of having to part from his family. Another reason was that he had been drinking since morning without having any food to forget his sorrow over this. Mother had prepared his favourite lemon rice and potato fry but he declined to have even that.

Turning to me, he said, "Hem, You know something. I have now got the true picture of my family down here. This time, I am going to do something for all of you. As soon as I find a job, I shall start sending you money. This time I am more determined than ever to make my family rich. You had taken care of my parents so lovingly. I shall repay all the loans that you have given me and my family. This is a promise. I could have ofcourse gone out and earned some money and helped my family tide over the financial crisis, but I did not like to leave my mother. I don't know if I would ever get this opportunity of being with my mother again. I really enjoyed staying beside my mother all these days!" As soon as I handed over the green stone studded silver ring and the black leather purse, he was so thrilled. He showed off the purse to everybody and demanded each of them to drop a few coins into it telling them, "this would remind me of you!" Mother secretly removed a hundred rupee note from her saving kit and dropped it into the purse. Babu was so happy and told her, "I would use this while returning from Jamaica next year!" Also he gleefully slipped the ring over his finger and flaunted around with it.

When it was time to leave, Babu prostrated at mother's feet and got her blessings. He then assured her, "mother, I would be sending rupees five thousand exclusively in your name and you can spend it as you wish!" Father never got tired of advising Babu. When Babu said good bye to him, once again father repeated his advice to him, "Your money is not important to us. You must give up drinking and smoking once you reach there. Take care of your health. Health is wealth! Don't forget that !"

Finally, Babu took my little son's hands into his and said, "Tarun, listen! Babu Uncle is leaving for Jamaica tonight. He may come back to India or he may die there in Jamaica itself !" While my little son did not comprehend its true purport and stood there bashfully peering into his face, his words sent a tremor across me. However, I remained silent without offering any comments. The fact that I had adhered to my vow of non-interference in his life, gladdened my heart!

61

A Gut Wrenching Pain

A great Tornado was raging in Jamaica at the time Babu landed there. Maureen had come to the airport to pick him up. He spoke to mother and Raghu for a long time on 15th September. He told mother that both his daughter and wife enjoyed the gifts that he had taken for them from India.

I had just come out from Babu mania. His short stay with us had temporarily got rid of the obssession I had over Babu and I decided to talk to him after a month.

It was on 25th September 2004, Saturday morning when I was reading out a story to my son that the phone rang. It was a long distance call and so I doubled over to pick it up, thrilled that Babu had himself called me. Infact it was very unusual of him to call me at this hour. He generally spoke to me in the night. As I lifted the phone, I was surprised to hear Maureen's voice. "How are you Maureen?", I asked. Her reply was vague and not clear to me. I always had difficulty understanding her accent. Unable to comprehend what she was saying, I continued, "Please give it to Sampath". While I waited anxiously to hear my brother's dashing voice, Maureen said, "Sampath has had a heart attack!" Her words were indistinct. They did not register in my mind or rather I pretended not to understand.With my heart racing, I reiterated my request, "please give it to Sampath no?" Maureen repeated the same words once again, "Sampath has had a heart attack!" Now, with a gut wrenching pain in my stomack, I shouted, "How is he now Maureen?" In a dismal and feeble voice, she said, "He is no more!" I was bewildered and not sure of what I was hearing. My mind became blank from shock. Anticipating the worst, I was momentarily paralyzed by a mixture of fear and anxiety and I once again asked in a pointblank manner, "is he alive or not Maureen?" "Sorry Hema! I just cannot help it. He is no more! He is not alive. He has left us!" I felt numb and sick to my stomach. It shook my entire system to the core. I wailed into the phone, Maureen, Maureen, Maureen. . . . . . . what are you telling me ? What are you telling me Maureen.? Before I could utter another word, the phone went dead.

The world around me started to collapse. My mind was completely shattered and momentarily I lost my capacity to think coherently. It was as though I was in the midst of an earthquake and every thing around me was falling to pieces. I was filled with utter shock and all I could do was to cry vociferously. Babu. . . . Babu. . . Babu. . . . I uttered his name loudly and cried. How did you have the mind to leave us all ? When are we going to see you again ? Is it for this I took so much pains to bring you back to India. I had been thinking of you day in and day out for the last nine years. I was all the while thinking that you would come back and take care of the family burdens and free me from every responsibilty. All my dreams have got shattered now!.

I then started running to the puja room. I wailed in a full throated voice in front of God. A vague and silly feeling crossed my mind then. Perhaps my hearfelt and plaintive renditions of my grief in front of Him would change His mind and He would bring my brother back to life! I pleaded with Him pitifully that this news must not be true !

And from time to time, ambiguous thoughts flashed in my mind. Am I having a bad dream ? A nightmare ? Did I hear correctly ? Hope it is not true! I longed that someone would phone up to me and tell me that my brother was alive. Crazy thoughts like these kept passing my mind continuously. I howled uncontrollably in front of God for a long time. "God, why did you do this to me ? What sin have I done to beget such a punishment in life! God, why did you separate my loving brother from me! Oh God, why did you give birth to me in this world if life was so meaningless. . . if we could not have any say in the things that were happening around us. . . . . are you so heartless ?

Though I knew from the very beginning that my brother was falling to pieces due to his addiction, I did not interfere in his life because I had to keep the promise I had given You on non-intereference! I believed that You would take care of him and I stuck to my guns and did not interfere in his life. Otherwise I could have once again offered my prayers in front of You seeking help for his relief from drinks. And at the time when I was contemplating on how best to thank You for bringing down my brother to India, and exempting me from the guilt that I was holding for nine long years, You have once again taken me to square one. I shall never become free from this guilt again! It shall always be alive in my heart. Nor is any consolation going to soothe my mind from the grief that has shrouded me presently.

I suddenly feel like a sinner, who has been punished enough by God for the wrong he has done! And what wrong have I done Oh God! Is it wrong to be greedy of money ? Is it wrong to have desires in life ? And if one suffers due to his karma done in the past, what have I done to beget such a punishment ? Is it wrong to love someone so dearly in life ? The rantings went on and on. . . . . . . But there were no answers from anyone! There was just silence in the room! Absolute silence! A deathly silence!

Unable to bear my howling, my husband entered the room. My tears glared my vision and I could see the hazy figure of my husband walking towards me. He admonished me to stop crying lest I hurt myself ! "What would happen to me and the children if you plan to cry your grief away in this manner ? I know it is very hard but try and control yourself ! That's life ! Everyone has to leave the world one day or the other!" The soothing words held no significance! His words got obscured and sunk deeply into an unknown realm of my mind as my body rocked uncontrollably from a fresh a break out of sobs!

62

Return of the Gift

The entire day I spent crying my grief away. It was beyond belief. Did I hear correctly ? Was it true ? I felt like I was trapped in a nightmare. It was not possible that Babu was gone. I prayed that what Maureen had just said was not true. I was overwhelmed by a constant wave of emotions of which I had no control. Powerful and disturbing thoughts criss-crossed my mind. Will I ever be able to come back to my usual self and be able to lead a normal life ? Will I be able to laugh or smile at people again ? Or even read a book or do any of the ordinary things that people did!

Why me ? How could God do this to me ? How could he shatter my life in this manner ? He has taken away my brother, whom I loved the most. No words of consolation could bring solace to my anguished mind. For nine long years, eversince I sent him to Jamaica, I had been thinking of him day in and day out. At first, it was the money that I was looking forward to from him. But when I realized that he was stranded and required help, I was dying to bring him back home safely. For nine long years, I had lived with the thought of my brother, hoping to see him. Finally, one day, I prayed to God that if he brings back my brother to India, I shall not interfere in his life again. And only after I took this vow of non-interference in my brother's life that my wish was fulfilled by God.

As a thanks giving to God, I firmly stuck to my vow of non-interference. When I saw my brother drinking and smoking nonstop, I was shell shocked. I knew from the very beginning that he was destroying his own life. His mind was turbulent and always in a state of unrest. For very often, while speaking to me, he would say, "Hem, I feel confused. I don't know what to do. When I reach Jamaica, I will have to start my life all over again. I may come back or I may not come back. I am not sure of anything ! " I would listen to his musings and smile silently but however not assure him that everthing was going to be fine and he did not have to worry. In fact, I was much overwhelmed with happiness that my brother was afterall sitting right in front of me, which mattered to me the most. This alone brought much satisfaction to me and I did not wish to get involved in his life again. His problems were no more of my concern. He is old enough to take care of himself. I had afterall prayed to God and brought him back to his parents and with that my job was over.

His foreboding words to my son, "Babu Uncle may come back to India or die there in Jamaica itself " sprang up to my mind. How brutal of me to have remained silent over his adverse statement ! Maybe I should have interfered in his life for one last time. I could have made a pact with God as usual and prayed for his drinking habit to stop. I could have counseled him and taken him to a rehabilitation centre and freed him from the vile habit which had destroyed him completely. I had made a promise to God and intended to keep it, no matter what. I had indeed committed a blunder in sticking firmly to my vow of non-interference in his life. While I was rejoicing at the reunion of my brother with the family and the fact that I had at last become free from the guilt bag that I had been carrying with me for nine long years, fate dealt a severe blow to me! Another wave of guilt feelings shafted through me once again. But this time, there will be no way out from the remorse, whatsoever !

Later during the day, when Raghu spoke to Maureen, she asked him if the body of Sam had to be sent to India. Raghu informed her that it was not necessary and that she could conduct the last rites in Jamaica itself. While talking to me about the customs and practices of the Jamaicans, Babu had dwelt at great length as to how they perform the funeral ceremony. They spend a lot of money for this purpose. The dead person is kept in a cold storage room for almost two weeks as a mark of honour and on the day of funeral, the entire Parish would accompany the body to the church for the last rituals.

Though Babu passed away on 24th September 2004, his funeral was performed only on the 9th of October 2004. His body was kept in the cold storage room for almost a fortnight. On the day of the funeral, I was sitting all alone mourning in silence visualizing the funeral procession. I recollected the talk we had just a few months back. With what gusto he had described the manner in which the funeral ceremony would be conducted in Jamaica! Only this time, it will be my own brother who is lying still and is being taken in the procession. Unbidden tears started flowing from my eyes. On seeing this, my little son ran up to me. Rubbing the tears, he asked, "are you crying because Sam has gone to the blue sky ? What will be in his big travel bag now ma?" His words invoked a fresh onslaught of tears. He never let the children touch his travel bag.

A few months later Maureen sent a parcel of things belonging to Sam, which she no longer required, alongwith the video of Babu's funeral ceremony. I did not have the heart to see the video then and have not seen it so far. I never will!

Of the items which Maureen had sent back to us, lay the valuable black leather purse which I had lovingly given to my brother before his departure to Jamaica. Words fail me and I can't put down on paper the agony I felt on seeing it.

63

The Guilt is Alive

Sam's death left a deafening silence in my life! I continued to remain in a state of shock for the next few weeks. Constantly struck with grief, I put on a gloomy appearance ; hardly speaking to anyone. I was blunt and indifferent to everything that was happening around me. I hated to even flash a smile or wish anybody. I expected people to know that something was really wrong with me. Something serious was bothering me and wished that they would stop by and enquire as to what exactly was wrong with me. Why had I changed from a person who would flash a ready smile to someone with a brooding look. But people were unmindful of others' feelings. For they were busy themselves in the rat race. In fact, they have become emotionally stone deaf, bogged down by problems of their own. They were unable to read my emotions. They had no empathy. I realized that unlike in the past, no one had the patience to sit down and listen to your woes.

I also realized that it was up to me to change myself and reset my life. Well, for the sake of my children and my husband who loved me a lot, I did not wish to continue brooding for the rest of my life wallowing in pain and self pity. I had to accept the reality that my brother was no more. The empathy I foolishly expected from the people around me is not going to change the situation I was presently in. My mental agony at the absence of my brother will not come to an end.

It was during this time, at the fag end of December 2004, that a catastrophe in the form of Tsunami rocked the world and shattered the lives of so many innocent people. Poignant stories of people who had lost their loved ones were continuously flashed on the television. I tried to identify myself with them. The story of one particular middle aged man, touched my heart and brought about a transformation in me. Scared out of their wits, his wife and two children clung to him for protection. Shortly, despite their strong grasp, they were caught up in the surging waters. With great horror, he saw his loved ones being gushed away in front of his eyes. He stood there rooted to the ground, wailing for help. Later, when the effects of Tsunami subsided, he made a frantic search of his family members. When at last, he realized that his search was futile, he broke down. However, this gentleman did not wish to be shrouded in misery and grief for the rest of his life. On the same day, he came across two children who were sitting alone and weeping over their lost parents. He brought meaning to his life by adopting the two orphaned children. He was an example to show that the human spirit is resilient and that no one can destroy it except yourself.

To me, he was my life changer. I consider him a heroic man who took his grief and sorrow in his stride, never losing courage or compromising his values. He changed his life for the better and his story changed my life too. I decided to adopt his powerful virtues for changing my life.

I too tried to come out of my grief. Afterall, death lays her icy hands on each and everyone of us. Nothing is permanent in this world and eventually, all of us will be gone one day. The life God has given me has to be lived, no matter what. Especially, when you have people you love and who love you in return. My husband and two children would not like to see me gloomy always. I did not wish to spread my sorrow to them. And that has been a very pretty tough decision that I had ever taken in my life.

I have still not lost faith in God. In fact, I did not like to start any unresolved argument with Him and abandon Him from my life. But now, I don't pray to Him for any thing! I am not interested in any of the worldy things anymore. Money, fame, riches, nothing at all! For, these can never bring back my loving brother!

The following lines from a poem written by an English Poet W. E. Henley, which I came across in *Reader's Digest* also stirred me.

"It matters not how straight the gate, how charged with punishments the scroll, I am the master of my fate. I am the captain of my soul."

Indeed! God has endowed us with an indomitable spirit. And no one can destroy this human spirit but yourself. When struck with any calamity, it has the power to recover from the shock ; rejuvenate itself and move on. For the first time, I tried to reconnect with the good feelings. One has to decide to be happy. I have resolved to be happy and tell myself that I should not let this sorrow dampen my spirits for the remaining part of my life. For we have got just one life to live!

However, despite the strong determination to change myself, the grip of guilt and anger had not begun to loosen. The guilt is still alive! Suffused with guilt and utterly devastated, I am now trying my best to find an escape within myself. To escape from the thoughts of Sam. And after a period of four years, I am gradually reviving from the shock. Day after day, the memory of Sam is slowly fading from my mind. And I am sure it will one day get completely erased out from my mind. And on that day, I shall be no more!

Epilogue

You must forgive the people you hate and not the people whom you love! Based on this theory, I have forgiven Narayanan, wherever in the world he is now ! In a way, he had tempted my brother and taken him to a foreign land and abandoned him heartlessly ; without feeling responsible for him. He had brought about a downfall of my brother and in turn of my whole family. However, I consider that this is all God's doing and we do not have any control over that. Like the victims of earthquake, Tsunami and bomb blasts, who lay down their lives for no fault of theirs and also have no say in the matter I have simply resigned to my fate cursing God alone.

I should have patiently listened to the musings of my father and ignored them silently like my other siblings. But out of deep and ardent affection I had for him, I had committed a blunder in going over-board in fulfilling all his desires. I was rather too naïve not to understand that grumbling was my father's innate trait. When at last realization struck me, it was too late.

I am filled with guilt once again. For I could have entered into a pact with God and prayed for my brother to stop his drinks and smoking habit. I had crazily stuck to my guns in following the vow of non-intereference in Babu's life. The guilt is alive and only this time I shall never become free from it.

Babu is now resting in peace. His state of prolonged anguish and turmoils are over. He has left us to suffer in mental agony for the rest of our lives. Our confusions of life begin. As for me, I miss Babu intolerably. I will never have the strength to recover from the grief over the absence of my brother. However, I will have to just keep living through it because that is life. The words "I have a loving sister" which he used frequently during his conversation with me keeps resonating in my ears.

This book is a tribute to his beloved daughter Krishna Kumar whom he referred to as the angel of his life. I seek salvation by talking to Krishna, from time to time and make it a point to send her a few Indian dresses every year on her birthday which she adores a lot.

Date : February, 2011 **Hemalatha Gnanasekar**

Index

N

O

P

Q

R